SINCE
THE
LAYOFFS

Also by Iain Levison

A Working Stiff's Manifesto

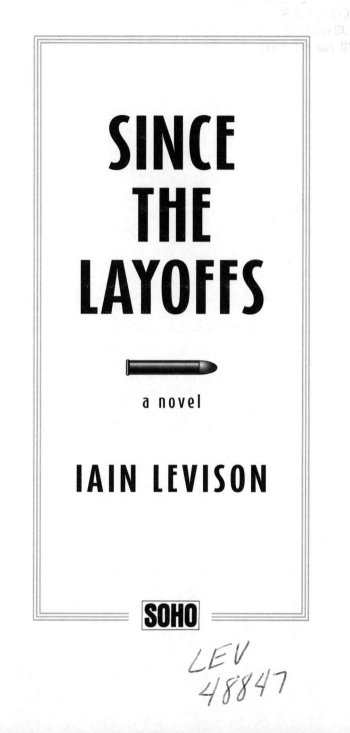

SINCE THE LAYOFFS

a novel

IAIN LEVISON

SOHO

Published by
Soho Press Inc.
853 Broadway
New York, NY 10003

Library of Congress Cataloging-in-Publication Data
Levison, Iain.
Since the layoffs : a novel / Iain Levison.
p. cm.
ISBN 1-56947-335-8 (alk. paper)
1. Young men—Fiction. 2. Unemployed—Fiction.
3. Criminals—Fiction. I. Title.
PS3612.E837S56 2003
813'.6—dc21   2002044654

10 9 8 7 6 5 4 3 2 1

To My Mother

Acknowledgments

I'd like to thank the following people who have given me help of one kind or another while I was writing this book:

Angela Hendrix, Kathleen Kern, Barbara Kingsbury, Andrew Langman, Travis MacCaskill, Faith Manney, Patricia Pelrine, Charles Rhyne, Nancy Santos, Marion Scepansky, Dave Snyder, Michael Taeckens, Jim Teal, and Nathan Watters.

ONE

I was in Tulley's, watching a Bills game with Tommy and Jeff
Zorda, and I had a hundred on the Bills to win. It was the third
quarter and the Bills were down 21-0 and didn't have any
offense to speak of, but this was back before we all got laid off, so
losing a C-note wasn't the end of the world. Anyway, there was this
TV behind Jeff's head that was showing the game about ten seconds ahead of all the other TVs, so I could see how each play was
going to turn out before the other two. I was just fucking around
at first, but I said, "Hey, I bet I can call the next five plays."

Tommy was interested just for fun, but Jeff Zorda, who had put
money on the Jets and was winning, had the gambling bug. "Ten
bucks a play. You have to call the players."

I had just wanted to play around, but whenever Jeff started winning he turned into a cocky prick who was always telling everyone
else they didn't know shit about football. So I took the bet.

"The next play'll be an end-around to Thomas. Right side."

"No way, dude," Zorda said. "It's third and six. They're not going to run it."

Sure enough, there was a right side end-around to Thomas for the first down. Zorda shrugged.

The next play was set up as a shotgun. Then one of the linemen moved and drew a penalty.

"This'll be a pass play, but it won't happen. The right tackle's going to move before the snap." I had given Zorda way too much information, a hint that I was cheating, but he didn't catch it. No matter how much you know about football, you can't predict a penalty. I don't think he was listening, as usual. Tommy figured something out right away and stuck his head over the booth and saw the other TV, but he didn't say anything. He just smiled. Tommy didn't care too much for Zorda. There were rumors about him and Tommy's wife.

Zorda watched the penalty and stared at me in admiration. "Damn. How the hell could you know that?" Still no suspicion.

"That tackle's been jiggling around the whole game," I said. "He was due for a penalty." Tommy smiled. "Next play'll be a screen pass to Taylor. He'll hit him underneath for a couple yards."

This went on for the whole five plays. I was just about to tell Zorda I was cheating when he got up, took a fifty out of his wallet and threw it at me. "Prick," he said. Then, much drunker than I realized, he staggered off to the bathroom, walking right past the TV that was showing the game ten seconds ahead.

"I'll tell him when he comes back," I said to Tommy.

"Fuck him."

But Zorda didn't come back. He met his coke dealer on the way to the bathroom and left the bar, sticking us with his tab. So Tommy and me split the fifty and used some of it to pay his tab, and Zorda got so fucked up he must have forgot all about it, because he never mentioned it at work.

And until I shot Corinne Gardocki in the head, that was the worst thing I had ever done for money.

Ken Gardocki is looking at some papers strewn around on his desk while I sit in his nip-and-tuck leather chair in my blue jeans and dungaree jacket, waiting for him to tell me what it is he wants. He has called me at seven this morning and asked me to come down to his office, mentioned a deal we could work out. Ken Gardocki is a bookie and I owe him somewhere in the neighborhood of forty-two hundred dollars so any kind of a deal sounds good. He knows I'm out of work, he knows everyone in this town is, but he still takes bets from me. Maybe he is going to ask me to paint his house, or run some errands for him. Maybe he needs a butler. I could do that. Anything to get me working again.

Ken Gardocki finds one of the papers he was looking for and holds it up, then looks at me thoughtfully. "Canadian football," he says.

"What?"

"You lost eighteen hundred dollars of your forty-two hundred on Canadian football."

"Yeah."

He laughs. "Tell me, Jake, can you name one player in the whole Canadian Football League?"

"Doug Flutie used to play for them."

"What was that, five years ago? He's with the Chargers now."

"Yeah." I like Ken Gardocki because he is a no-bullshit guy. He is also the only guy in town making money, because he sells drugs and guns and he is a bookie. In a town where three-quarters of the men have been laid off in the last nine months, the businesses of desperation are booming.

But I am beginning to wonder why I've been called here. Does he need someone to do a few chores for him, or what? Is it really necessary to go back through my betting history? Obviously, the list of my bets contains a few errors in judgment, or I wouldn't be here in the first place.

"How do you even find out the scores to a Canadian Football League game? ESPN doesn't run them. How do you find out any scores, for that matter, now that your cable has been cut off?"

"You know my cable was cut off?"

Gardocki shrugs. "Everybody's cable is getting cut off." He flips through some other papers and then throws the stack on the desk and looks at me. "So you're placing bets on Canadian football and you can't name a CFL player. What does that tell me?"

Where the fuck am I, in the principal's office? Am I about to be given detention for losing bets? "I don't know, Ken. What does it tell you?"

"It tells me you're desperate."

I shrug.

"It tells me you're betting for the money."

"As opposed to what?"

"As a hobby. For the action. You're betting to feed yourself. You need to place a bet to get the idea that you're making cash, just like you did before the layoffs."

"Yeah. That sounds about right."

Gardocki nods. "You want a beer?"

"It's ten in the morning, Ken. I'm unemployed and I have a gambling problem. I'm not a drunk."

Gardocki nods and smiles. That's the reason people like him, the reason I like him, because he smiles a lot. He is in his mid-fifties, and he has no virtues, and he doesn't take shit from people and he smiles a lot and he is probably the richest man in town, now that the guys who owned the factory have left. Gone to Texas, or Mexico, or Hollywood. Some place with more sun and cheaper labor than here.

"How much more time have you got left on benefits? Before the government cuts you off?"

I figure now that we're going somewhere with this. He's leading up to something, maybe he's going to ask me to be one of his
henchmen. Hell, I could do that. Drop coke and weed off at people's doors. Maybe he'll let me drive one of his SUVs. I could cruise
around town and listen to CDs and bring people their daily drug
shipments, for which they would exchange their unemployment
checks. I don't have a problem with that. Somebody will be doing
it whether I say yes or no. My moral refusal won't suddenly put a
halt to this shattered town's substance abuse problem. Something
like that would tide me over, until the new factory opened. They
were already talking about a new factory.

"One year and three months."

"Then what? You going to starve to death in your apartment?"

"The new factory'll have opened by then."

Gardocki shakes his head. "There's not going to be any new factory. Who the hell would want to open a factory here?"

"I heard Scott Paper was looking at the location." Tommy had
called me up and told me he'd read that in the paper. Big businesses were interested, I knew that. There was a pool of skilled
workers, a building already set up to produce machine-tooled
parts for tractors. Just a few changes, and it would be up and running, producing something else. We all knew that.

Gardocki laughs again. "Scott Paper." He shakes his head. "That
was a heavy metal factory. You think they're going to turn it into
a paper mill? And go through all that union bullshit again? Nobody
wants to deal with unions anymore. They want Mexicans. They
want people who'll appreciate seven dollars an hour, not gripe
about seventeen. The factory days here are over, Jake." He leans
back in his chair and lights a cigarette. "What happened to that
pretty little girl you were going around with?"

"Fuck you."

Gardocki adopts an expression of surprise. "Is that off limits?"

"You know my cable's cut off, but you don't know my girlfriend
moved out?"

"She went off with some used car dealer, huh?" Gardocki is looking sympathetic, so as not to rile me more.

"He was a new car dealer."

After the factory closed, the car dealerships had left town, too. Jobless people don't buy a lot of new cars. Kelly had gone with him, to Ypsilanti. Before she left there had been a lot of agonizing, when she went through her touching "What should I do?" phase. Kelly never asked herself what she should do when I was making seventeen dollars an hour. After her seven-dollar-an-hour salary as a receptionist at a car dealership made her the top grosser of the household, I noticed she began asking herself these deep philosophical questions. She told me some salesman was asking her to go to Ypsilanti with him, and whatever should she do? I told her to fuck off, and went and placed a bet on Canadian Football. After she moved out, I never picked up the phone, didn't return the one letter I got from her and didn't say goodbye. Someone new would come along, once the new factory opened.

"Jake, I want you to kill my wife."

I laugh. Then I search Gardocki's face for signs of humor. But I don't see any. Gardocki isn't even looking at me. He is looking at a spot on the wall above my head, expressionless. He smokes his cigarette and stares, waiting for it to sink in.

"I'm not going to kill your wife, Ken."

Gardocki nods. "What *are* you going to do? Go back to your one-bedroom apartment? Hang around all day? Walk from one end of town to the other, then spend three hours sitting in the library? Go down and see your friend Tommy at the convenience store where he works, and have him steal you a pack of cigarettes?" That was eerie. He knows I have Tommy steal me cigs from the convenience store, but it isn't really stealing because Tommy is the manager and he knows I can't afford them so he just lets me have them. How long has Gardocki been following me, collecting information on me?

"You're going to get evicted eventually, you know that? And what are you going to do then? Become homeless?" Gardocki is being conversational now, and he offers me a cigarette. It is almost a relief for me to hear these words spoken, the same words I hear going through my head twenty-four hours a day. What are you going to do for work? How are you going to pay bills? Every month, I lose another possession to the pawn shop or the repo man. I've already lost the 1997 Dodge Viper and replaced it with a 1980 Honda Civic. How much more room is there to downgrade, before I come home to an empty apartment? One day I'll come home and the locks will be changed. Then what? THEN WHAT? I try to quieten the voices with anything I can get my hands on, but these aren't the voices of a crazy person. These voices make sense.

"What are you going to do about your gambling debt, Jake?"

"Jesus, Ken, you make this sound like a career opportunity."

Gardocki nods and smiles. He offers me the smoke, and I take it. He goes and stands by the dirty window that looks out over a frozen field and a few rusted shacks.

"Six hundred people, out of work, collecting government cheese," he says, his voice foggy. "I could make this offer to all of them and at least twenty would say yes. Don't you think?" He turns around and looks at me.

"I don't know."

"Think of the men you used to work with. I mean really think of them. The ones with families, the ones with little children going to that dump of an elementary school. Think of your friend Tommy, managing a fucking convenience store, for what, seven-fifty an hour? He's got a kid, doesn't he?"

"Tommy wouldn't do it."

"How the fuck do you know? Five thousand for one day's work? I think you start throwing those numbers around in this town and you'd find there are a lot of people would do things. It'd pay Tommy's mortgage, wouldn't it?"

"Five thousand?" I just say that before I can stop myself, and I notice behind Gardocki's eyes the instant flash of triumph. In that millisecond, when I am thinking about the money and not about my soul, or morality, or what my mother would say if she were still alive, he knows he's won. That would be the gambling debt gone PLUS eight hundred dollars. Eight hundred dollars cash. I hadn't seen that much money in nine months. I could go to a bar and pay my tab with cash. I could buy milk and bread and make sandwiches and buy real cheddar instead of that government crap that was giving me the shits. I could get my TV back from the pawn shop and get the cable hooked up again and have people over. I could talk to Kelly again, maybe drive down to Ypsilanti and take her out to dinner. Why did I just think that? Fuck Kelly. But I *could* do it, if I felt like it, if I had eight hundred dollars.

Then I think of Jeff Zorda. "Zorda would do it," I say. "Zorda would do it in a heartbeat."

"Yes, he would," Gardocki agrees, and for a second, I think a funny expression flashes across his face. "But I picked you."

"Why me?" I ask.

"Because I like you."

"Bullshit. You think I'm evil, or something."

"No." Gardocki sits back down again. "I think I can trust you. You're smart, too. You're the type of guy who really needs this offer, but wouldn't go around telling everyone if you decided not to do it. Plus, you're not married. Nobody to go and agonize over the decision to. No wife that I have to worry about whether or not you told. Men tell women everything in bed, and you're not getting laid." He laughs, then goes serious again. "You do what you got to do to survive, Jake. These are tough times."

Who could argue with that? The cops? The preacher? I hadn't been to church since the layoffs. The cops and preachers had jobs, anyway. Their arguments were meaningless.

"Why do you think I kept taking your bets? I cut off everyone else a long time ago."

"I did wonder that."

"This *is* a career opportunity, Jake. And it might be your last fuckin' one."

"I'll do it."

Gardocki nods. He tells me he'll pick me up later and we'll go for a ride. He tells me to wear nice clothes. He hands me five twenty-dollar bills.

I walk out of the office and get back in my car, not with the heavy heart of a man who has agreed to compromise all his values, but with the soaring high of a man who has gotten a job.

"Here's how it's going to work," Gardocki says.

We are at La Cocina, a pricey Italian restaurant nearly a half-hour from town. I haven't had a decent meal in months, and I'm paying more attention to the menu than to anything else around me. I can't believe my luck. This morning, I woke up expecting another day of nothing, and tonight I'm at a classy restaurant having gnocchi appetizers and a bottle of Merlot. Even if I bailed out of the whole thing, I'd still have this meal to remember.

"Next Saturday," Gardocki says, "eight days from now, I'm going out of town for the weekend. I've got a friend in Denver I'm going to go visit."

"Okay," I tell him. I pour myself another glass of wine.

"My wife will be home that night. She always stays home on Saturdays. It's my night out. She's having an affair with an airline pilot, and he's always in town. He's going to have to leave about nine o'clock. Plane to catch. You go in through the back door, shoot her with this gun I'm going to give you, and walk home."

"The back door will be open?"

"Doesn't close right. We live up a dirt road about a mile from anywhere, so I haven't bothered fixing it. No crime out that way." He smiles to himself. "Until Saturday. If you have to make noise, that's fine. Don't let her get a phone call off to the police first, that's really your only concern."

I nod.

"I've been planning this for eight months, Jake. I've got everything figured out."

"That's very reassuring."

"You're the guy for the job. From day one, I knew it had to be you."

I find this flattering. Being considered the ideal hit man might not seem like a compliment to most people, but to a man who has been out of work for nine months, having someone respect you for any reason is high praise. That's what you miss most about work. There's the money, of course, but it's also the idea that you are worth something to someone. When you miss a day, people call your house to find out where you are. If I died in my apartment now, I'd be pretty smelly before anyone came looking. Probably Tommy, who'd have noticed I hadn't been around to steal cigarettes in a while.

"You also have to make sure no one finds you on the way home. Don't smoke outside my house and leave cigarette butts around. They can do things now with DNA, all that shit. Don't leave boot prints in my house, either. Wrap rags around your feet so they can't get a clear boot print, especially if it's snowing."

The waitress comes up and brings our food, and Gardocki changes the subject so deftly it leaves me worried. He's too good at deception, and I'm in a life-or-death pact with him. "And Favre, I'm not sure how much longer he's going to last. The Packers now aren't the same Packers we saw in the Super Bowl two years in a row." He says this in the same voice he has just used talking about the murder of his wife. The waitress tells us to enjoy our meal and walks off, and Gardocki continues, without missing a beat, "I've got your gambling stuff worked out, too."

"How do you mean?" I stare at my steaming bowl of baked ziti, fork ready.

"I'm leaving a line blank on my betting sheets. You're going to place a fifty-eight hundred dollar bet on the Jets-Bills game this Sunday. Whoever wins, I'll just fill that in as your bet. Minus the vig, I'll owe you exactly five grand. That's how you explain coming into the money to everyone you know."

I nod.

"Do you have any problems with this?"

"I understand everything. I'll do a good job."

"That's not what I mean."

"Problems? You mean moral problems?"

"Yeah." Gardocki is waiting to tear into his food, but is staring at me patiently.

"Yes."

Gardocki nods. "Good," he says. "Good answer. If you'd said no, I'd know you were lying. Do you think these problems are going to stop you from doing a good job?"

"No."

"We'll talk about the deeper issues later. For now, just kill my wife and we'll all be happier."

We begin to eat.

I have lied to Ken Gardocki. I don't have any moral problems.

I was aware the question was loaded when he asked, that he was looking for a specific answer. I knew he knew me well enough to suspect I would be morally torn, and I wanted to appear predictable to him, safe. I didn't want Gardocki's big fear to be that I will suddenly find Jesus when I am standing in the kitchen, pointing the gun at his wife's head. I have a feeling I'm going to do a much better job than he thinks. I might discover hidden talents.

The fact is, my morality is all but gone. My own life was taken from me by a twist of fate, an economic whim, a stroke of a pen in some office in New York City. My town is destroyed, my girlfriend is gone, my friends and I are constantly broke. Somebody killed me and my town, and I'm sure they're not tossing and turning about it. Why should I tear my hair out over Corinne Gardocki?

Killing other people, now the idea has been broached, doesn't seem like that much of a stretch. Corinne Gardocki. I've never met the woman. What little I know about her comes from barroom rumors. About five years ago, I placed a bet with Gardocki in a bar, and afterwards got to drinking with some of his older acquaintances. They were all guys from the factory, metal workers who were just a few months from retirement, and the conversation this night turned to Gardocki's new wife, Corinne. She was a stripper at a so-called gentleman's club up Highway 40, and Gardocki had laid eyes on her one night and determined that she would be his next wife, replacing the one who had passed away from cancer some six years before. Gardocki had been infatuated, had bought her all kinds of presents and visited her constantly. After the stripper's don't-appear-too-eager mandatory nine-week waiting period, she became his wife.

The conversation at the bar that night had been mostly derisive of the new Gardocki marriage. Most of the metalworkers were laughing about it, making jokes about her fucking ole Ken to death and then keeping his plush new house, the product of twenty years of factory work and twenty years of bookmaking. Most of these older guys said they didn't trust her. They talked about how sweet Ken's first wife had been and how reptilian this one was in comparison. At the time, I figured it was just jealousy. Now, having entered into a contract to kill her only five years later, evidently these older guys had seen something that Gardocki had missed.

Maybe none of it is true. Maybe Corinne Gardocki spends her days volunteering at the homeless shelter and the affair with the airline pilot is a product of Gardocki's aging paranoia. Maybe the "airline pilot" is her brother. The fact is, it doesn't matter much to me. She is going to die because I have been laid off from a profitable factory in the middle of my career. She is going to die because my girlfriend left me because I can't deal with life in the unemployment line. Corinne Gardocki is a dead woman because some Wall Street whiz kid decided our factory could turn a higher profit if it was situated in Mexico. Catch you later, Corinne. Any moral problems? Not really.

* * *

I go down and see Tommy at the convenience store, and he has great news for me.

"Jake, one of my counter kids got shot last night," he tells me. "We've got a job opening here."

Yesterday, this would have been great news. Yesterday, I would have started crying with gratitude that Tommy had offered me, had reserved for me, the $5.75 an hour position as a convenience store clerk. Today, I don't know what to say, because I have ninety-seven dollars in my pocket and I had gone down there to have Tommy steal me cigs so he would think I was still broke. I couldn't let anybody know I had money until after the supposed bet went down, when there would be a legitimate explanation. So my plan had been to continue my usual broke behavior for the rest of the week. Now this creates a problem. If I say I'll take the job, and Tommy needs me Saturday night, how do I kill Corinne Gardocki if I have to work at a convenience store?

Tommy mistakes my silence for glee-related shock, and he tells me the story of the shooting. Apparently, the cops came last night to haul off one of Tommy's two employees, who was trafficking marijuana and cocaine out of the store. He had been squealed on by some kid who had been busted with an eighth, and when the cops came for him he grabbed a gun the store stashed under the counter and ran off through the parking lot. One of the cops saw him with the gun and winged him. If my cable wasn't cut off I might have seen this on the news, if the newspeople even bothered reporting stuff like this any more.

"That's great, Tommy," I say, my voice lacking the required enthusiasm. I have eight hundred dollars coming to me, I don't need to be wearing an apron and making coffee for truck drivers and forking over cigs to housewives for three fifty a pack. But Tommy looks delighted for me. So I've gone from having nothing to do all day to having to juggle my schedule. "When do you want me to start?"

"Today would be great. Come back at five. I can probably squeeze you in as an assistant manager. That's six fifty an hour."

"Great, thanks, man. I appreciate it." I know that the kid who got shot, the drug dealer, was the one who worked the overnight shift. So Tommy's probably going to expect me to work overnight Saturday, and I have to make up an excuse to get Saturday off. But what excuse can I use? Tommy knows I'm broke and have nothing to do, ever. I couldn't afford a date even if I had one, and Tommy knows all the girls I know, so even if I said I was going out with one he'd mention it to her if he saw her. Now this is getting complicated.

I need someone to vouch for me as being busy Saturday so I can request it off. The obvious choice is Ken Gardocki, but he's going to be out of town. Besides, it's best if I use Gardocki's name as little as possible in the next few weeks, and limit my contact with him. Even if Gardocki provides me with an alibi, that'll look worse than no alibi at all because the alibi could obviously be traced back to Gardocki. All this is going through my mind as I stare, with an expression of forced joy, at Tommy.

It dawns on me for the first time that being a contract killer is more than just pulling a trigger.

"Hey, man, can I borrow a pack of smokes until my first paycheck?"

Tommy nods and grins. He gets them for me. Then he slaps me on the shoulder. "You and me, man. Workin' together again."

I get home just as the phone is ringing, and as my mind is buzzing with thoughts of my new career, I answer it without first checking the caller ID. It is a debt collector, one of many I have been avoiding lately.

"Mr. Jake Skowran?" I realize immediately I have made a mistake.

"Yes, this is me." I make another one. When in debt, never admit to being yourself on the phone.

"This is Mike Murty from Consolidated Finances." His voice is cold and humorless. I hate that, the rudeness with which they begin. I swear, if there was a single one of these guys who didn't forgo the formalities, who chatted with me for a bit, asked me how my day was going, I'd almost be tempted to care that I owed their company a lot of money. "You have a $3,189.66 outstanding balance on your Visa account, and we haven't had a payment from you for four months. What are you going to do about that?"

"Hold on," I say. "Let me get a cigarette." I fumble around, find my lighter, light the cigarette, exhale, and sit down on the couch. Mike Murty waits patiently. "Now, what were you saying?"

He repeats the same information in the same tone, and asks me the same question. What am I going to do about it? I don't know. Get used to it eventually, I guess.

"I've been out of work for nine months," I tell him. "I got laid off. Everyone in my town got laid off."

There is a silence.

"Mr. Skowran," he says. "This debt isn't going to go away. We need some kind of payment, something to show good faith. Then we can set you up with a payment plan."

"I'm on unemployment," I tell him.

"Unless you can give us something, we're going to have to file a judgment against you. That's going to effect your credit . . . ."

He rambles on. I'm not listening. I lie down on the couch and look at the dust outline where my TV used to be. The entertainment center is empty, the stereo gone, too. I can see my breath frosting up into the cool air. The heat has been cut off. Some guy in an office hundreds of miles away writing bad things about me on a computer is the least of my problems.

"I'd like a promise from you that we can expect at least one hundred dollars by the end of the month or we're going to have to take action," he says.

Something comes over me. I am a contract killer now, I don't have to take shit from anyone. I have a job, I'll be coming into money soon. I'm not going to spend another day avoiding people

because I owe them money. I owe *them,* they want to talk to *me.*
This is a position of strength.

"Do you remember elementary school?" I ask him.

There is a pause, then he says, "Mr. Skowran? I asked about a
payment."

"I asked you if you remembered elementary school."

"Mr. Skowran, I'd like to stay on the subject here. Are you or are
you not going to be able—"

"Because I wanted to know if this was it."

He is curious now. "If this was what?"

"Is this what you dreamed of doing when you were in elementary school? Was this your little boy's daydream? Did you stare out
of the window of your first grade class and think, one day, one of
these days, I'm going to call up people who have been laid off and
pester the fuck out of them so they could give their unemployment
checks to a giant corporation that charges TWENTY-SIX FUCKING
PERCENT INTEREST PLUS LATE FEES . . . ."

The phone is dead. Mike Murty doesn't want to hear my irrational
screaming. Mike Murty has other people to torment. Maybe there
is an unwed mother somewhere in Tennessee he can convince to
send him half her food stamps. But me, I feel good. For the first
time in months, I feel powerful. All the fear and worry have turned
into a hard core of hate, and it has a life of its own.

Jake Skowran is back.

TWO

A sixteen-year-old kid named Jughead shows me around the Gas'n'Go and explains how to use the cash register while Tommy goes home for dinner. He doesn't make eye contact with me once and he mumbles, but fortunately Tommy has provided me with a corporate pamphlet which outlines my responsibilities. I can't understand anything Jughead says, but things are easy to figure out. The Gas'n'Go uses a scanner for everything, so I don't have to know prices, and the register totals everything. My main job is to make sure people don't shoplift or try to shoot me.

Because of the events of last night, the gun which the store usually keeps behind the counter is in a police evidence room, so if anyone does try to shoot me, the plan, I gather, is for me to try to conceal my main arteries. I'm also supposed to be comforted by the fact that surveillance cameras, with which the Gas'n'Go is liberally

17

sprinkled, will catch people in the act of shooting me. The fact that the surveillance tapes are in an unlocked room which anyone could get to by stepping over my body makes the whole forty thousand dollar system worthless, to my mind, but this is corporate security. This is them taking care of us.

Before the factory closed, there wasn't a single armed robbery in this town for as long as I can remember. Since the layoffs, the late-night convenience stores have become fortresses, the six-dollar-an-hour nightshift workers there the equivalent of combat veterans. Every one of them can tell a story of a gun battle. Jughead doesn't seem the least bit fazed by hearing the police have just gunned down his co-worker. When I ask him about it, he shrugs and says, "Agasta mel."

"What?"

"I gotta stock milk. Washaresta."

"Watch the register?"

"Yeah." He is gone.

I sit by the register and read my pamphlet, a nineteen-page tiny-print roman à clef describing the exciting and rewarding career on which I have just been launched. The cover shows a stunning blonde wearing a Gas'n'Go uniform smiling broadly as she hands change to a well-dressed, beaming customer. Inside, I learn it is only a matter of time before I move up the Gas'n'Go food chain to become regional director of all the Gas'n'Gos in the Midwest.

A car pulls up, an old orange BMW covered with rust spots. I eagerly await my first customer, but before I can pleasantly welcome him to Gas'n'Go, Jughead comes out from the back and says, "Reddonplay."

"What?"

"You gotta write down the plate."

"What plate?"

Jughead is clearly irritated with me. He pushes past me and pulls out from under the counter a small keyboard. He looks at a tiny color video monitor and types in the car's license plate number, then puts the keyboard back. "All old cars," he tells me. "Anything suspicious."

"You think he's suspicious?"

"It's an old car."

"But he's already on the monitor. If he does anything the cops'll get him."

Jughead reaches down and shows me the keyboard, which is hooked into the wall with a thick black cord. "Gusta cops," he says. It goes to the cops.

Miraculous. Modern technology at its best. When I type in a plate number, the plate is run through a police computer. If it's a stolen car, or a car registered to someone with an outstanding bench warrant, a police car is immediately and automatically dispatched to the Gas'n'Go. Jughead stares fondly at the keyboard. He finds this technology intriguing, and it gives him a sense of comfort. For my part, all I see is the increased likelihood of a shoot-out right in the store. I make a mental note never to use this feature.

The customer, a middle-aged, potbellied, unshaven man with grease on his hands, comes in and hands Jughead a five dollar bill for $2.97 in gas. He doesn't look at either of us. Jughead doesn't look at him as he hands him $2.03. No words are exchanged as the man leaves, pushing the glass door open with his blackened hands, smudging the glass.

"Yagattaclindor," Jughead says, as he goes back to stocking the milk. I gotta clean the door. "Agasta mel."

Jughead goes home at seven because there's a state law prohibiting minors from working at night. The only other employee on Tommy's roster was shot last night. So tonight, that leaves me here until seven in the morning, a fourteen-hour shift for someone who doesn't have any idea how anything in the store works.

I wonder if the Gas'n'Go CEOs are aware that things like this occur, their hundred thousand dollar business left in the hands of the likes of Jughead and myself. Judging by their pamphlet, I'd guess not. I think they honestly believe that we smile a lot and wear pressed uniforms and our customers are full of delight. I'm wearing torn three-year-old jeans and I'm happy if the people I hand change to don't have guns. I wonder how this division began, the line between the pamphlet and reality. Did the suits who wrote this never visit one of their stores? Perhaps it's just this store, in this wrecked town, which is an embarrassment to the Gas'n'Go empire. I suspect not. I suspect all of America is slowly sinking into moral and financial decay while the pamphlet-writers sit in their offices with a view of rivers or valleys and make a sport of pretending not to notice. What difference does it make to them, unless there is actually a revolution? This pamphlet was written to pacify stockholders. I tear it into small pieces in front of a surveillance camera, and as the hours pass, I tear the pieces smaller still, until, by three in the morning, I have confetti, and by sunrise, dust.

Throughout the night I get customers and I learn things. An overweight woman in her fifties with unwashed, stringy black hair comes in at two in the morning and buys three gallons of whole milk. She hands me what looks like a credit card, but instead of a bank logo, this is plain white and has a faded government seal on it. I look at her suspiciously.

"Run it," she says.

I shrug and swipe it through the credit card machine. Nothing happens. She looks at me, I look at her.

"Are you new?" she asks me. She is wheezing with the effort of carrying the milk to the counter.

"Yeah."

"That's an EFS card. You have to push the EFS button on the machine." She smiles at me patiently.

I figure she's a mental patient, and this card is probably an access card to a parking garage in Iowa. I decide to let her have the milk. She obviously likes milk a lot and we've got plenty.

"It's okay," I tell her. "Just take the milk."

"There's a switch, an EFS switch," she says, getting impatient, or annoyed at being treated like a charity case. Then I see a tiny switch at the bottom of the credit card machine marked "EFS." I click the switch, and I'm amazed when a receipt prints up. She signs a copy and walks off, limping under the weight of three gallons of milk which she appears to be carrying home through the cold. It must be for a family's breakfast. I look at the receipt, and it says, "Electronic Food Stamps, Inc."

Electronic Food Stamps, Incorporated. Not Electronic Food Stamps, but Electronic Food Stamps, Incorporated. This is a business. Somebody's making money designing ways to get government aid to people who have been tossed aside. Some money grubbing software designer has a government contract because we all lost our jobs.

That's the biggest insult of all, that we are being fed off. The destruction of my life, my town, represents a business opportunity to someone else. Nine months ago, this woman walking through the cold was probably a factory employee, or perhaps the wife of one, and her children had health insurance and she had a car and she bought milk in the daytime, with money. I am suddenly filled with the urge to find the fucker who owns this EFS company and shoot him right in the fucking face. I feel that someone owes me an explanation, not a corporate public relations-type explanation, but a down-on-your-knees-begging-for-your-life explanation, which is the only kind worth listening to.

But he's not the only one. From now on, I have to make a list of people who need to be shot in the face. There needs to be a real bloodbath, to equal the financial and emotional one which has just been drawn for all of us.

Tommy comes in at six thirty and puts coffee on and looks around. During the night I have mopped the floor three times, cleaned all the glass, scrubbed the coffee pots and polished every inch of stainless steel.

"The place looks good, Jake," he says. "How do you like it so far?"

"It's easy enough."

"Does the night shift bother you?"

"I'll get used to it."

"Got any questions about anything?"

"How do you understand Jughead?"

Tommy laughs. "He's a good kid. He's worked here since his dad got laid off at the plant. Jughead's the only person in the family with a job."

"Who was his dad?"

"A truck driver. Johnny something. Prezda, that's it. Johnny Prezda. You remember him?"

I think back. I can't remember much about the factory, the faces fade away more each day. It has become a distant memory, and sometimes I walk around and wonder if there ever really was a factory, a center to this town. Did we ever all get off work at five on Friday afternoons and head over to Tulley's and drink and laugh and debate whether or not to split an eight ball of coke? Did I ever have a girlfriend named Kelly who was beautiful and sweet, and did she and I ever go for long walks at night when it was starting to rain and talk about having children and what kind of car to buy? I shake my head. "I don't remember him."

Tommy shrugs. "See you at five?"

"Five it is."

On my walk home, I pass Kristy's, the breakfast place where Kelly and I used to go on Sunday mornings. There was usually a line out the door by nine o'clock. The place still isn't boarded up, but I can tell it soon will be. There are three cars in a parking lot that was built for one hundred. A black man in a shoddy jacket with a worn woolen cap is waiting outside the front door to beg customers for change, but there aren't any.

A freezing rain has started, and the man calls to me. "Hey pardner, can you spare some change? I'm trying to catch a bus."

I know this is a lie and I don't care. He's bummed money off me maybe twenty times and he never remembers me. He's been saving up to catch this bus for several years now. It must be an expensive fare. I've snagged a few quarters from the register during the night, and I give them to him.

"Thanks, man." He takes the quarters and points to Kristy's, behind him. "Don't nobody come here no more."

"Costs money, man. Nobody's got any."

"'Cause the factory closed?"

"I figure."

"I gotta get out of this town."

"Good luck with that."

I walk home and think about a guy from the plant I used to work with named Tim Gregg. He was forty-six and he had a wife and two children, and about a month after the factory closed, because I was a department manager, the company sent me to a list of employee's houses to make sure they had begun receiving a government benefit. It was three days' work, so I took it. Gregg was the last person on my list for that day, and when I got to his house, I found him in the garage attaching a rubber hose to his exhaust pipe. He looked pale. He had been trying to asphyxiate himself in his garage, only the hose had come off and the garage was worn and full of holes and didn't make for much of a gas chamber. He was working on the problem when I showed up, and tried to act as if he was just tidying up the place.

"Tim, man," I said to him. "Are you trying to kill yourself?"

He just sat and looked at me and didn't say anything. Then he signed the papers I needed him to sign and he waited for me to leave, so that he could go back to finishing himself off. I wouldn't leave.

"You can go now," he said.

I knew I couldn't leave. If I heard about him dead the next day I knew I wouldn't be able to live with myself. And I couldn't call the cops, because all the cops ever did around here was give people DUIs and generally piss on you. Nobody in my town called the cops, it just wasn't something you did. So I hung out, and we talked about sports. After a while, he realized I wasn't going to leave, at least not until he yanked the rubber tubing out of the exhaust pipe and opened up all the garage doors. We talked for a couple of hours, never touching on any subject like the plant closing. It was mostly about Brett Favre or Elway. Then he started undoing stuff while we were talking, pulling duct tape off the holes in the roof and unplugging the hose from the exhaust. Then his wife came home, and I chatted with her for a bit, then left.

The last I'd heard of the Greggs, they had moved to Minneapolis to live with Tim's mother.

The thing I remember about it is talking to him, thinking, I don't even know this guy. I've never worked a shift with him, but I'm going to make it a point to see that he doesn't kill himself. I'm going to look after him, if only for a day, because he's not a whole lot different from me. What he does after today, that's his business, but he's not killing himself with me standing here pretending it isn't happening.

That decency in me is gone now, along with the Greggs and the factory. If I showed up at his house today and he had a noose around his neck and a gun in his mouth, I'd just get the signature and be gone in time not to hear the shot. I gave the bum some quarters because I had them in my pocket, but if he spends it on bad smack and is rotting in an alley by the time I get home, I don't care. If he catches the mythical bus and reunites with his loved ones after years of begging for change outside Kristy's, I don't care. Either is fine with me.

I don't care anymore. You got your problems and I got mine.

I go to sleep on my couch, exhausted for the first time in months, exhausted from doing a job, from working and earning money. The sleep is sweet and refreshing. I am wakened from it at about ten in the morning by a phone call from Denise at Consolidated Financial.

Denise has a voice so gentle and sexy she should be working a different kind of 1-800 number. The people at Consolidated Financial must have thought, after I screamed at Mike Murty, that they could catch more flies with honey. It works. I'm so relaxed and surprised to hear a sweet female voice on the phone that I don't hang up, even after she introduces herself as an agent of the collection service.

"The reason I'm calling, Mr. Skowran, is that we have an outstanding debt to resolve," she says, only she's making it sound sexy. Resolve my debt, baby, oh yeah. "If you don't take care of this, you could have some difficulty down the road."

"Like what?" I ask sleepily.

"Well, it could be difficult for you to buy a house."

"Buy a house?"

"Yes," she continues. "It would be difficult to have a mortgage application accepted with this on your credit record . . . ."

And I'm off.

"Lady, I make SIX FIFTY A FUCKING HOUR IN A GOD-DAMNED CONVENIENCE STORE!!! DO YOU THINK I GO HOUSE SHOPPING ON MY DAYS OFF? DO YOU HONESTLY THINK THAT PEOPLE MAKING SIX FIFTY AN HOUR—" I hear a dial tone. These people called me and aggravated me on a FUCKING SUNDAY MORNING! Don't they ever rest? Is nothing sacred?

No, it isn't. Not around here. No church for me. I remember the week the news of the layoffs hit, they had a minister come and tell us that if anyone wanted to talk, he'd be there for them. A bunch of guys went down to talk to him, and they came back and told the same story. The reverend apparently had his own agenda. He was a minister hired by the company, sent in from New York. They flew in a minister to make sure nobody was going to show up the next day with an M-16 and start mowing down people in Personnel, which had happened when they closed a plant in Kansas. As for providing actual comfort, he couldn't have cared less. He was mostly interested in our gun collections.

Now, when the people around here go to church, they do so
with the sense that they have pissed God off, and are trying to make
things right again. They don't go out of gratitude for their blessings,
but out of a fear that things will get even worse if they don't start
groveling to a higher power in a hurry. Nobody wants lightning
bolts or floods slamming into them as they shuffle back from the
unemployment office.

Tonight is my second and final day of training with Jughead. After
this, I'll be left on my own. Because it is Sunday night, Jughead
explains in his mumbling dialect, tomorrow morning will be much
busier than last night, so I have more setting up to do. People will
be coming in early to buy cigarettes, get coffee and gas, maybe
microwave a sticky bun on their way to jobs they still have. We're
close to a highway. Truckers passing through often stop by, and
the coffee machines have to be filled and ready to go. Even
though it is illegal, Jughead has worked a few overnight shifts and
he shows me some tricks and shortcuts.

"Allscontdadror early," he tells me. Always count my drawer
early, so I don't have to do it when people start showing up at
around six a.m. The drawer I count at five will be the one Tommy
uses on the day shift. He shows me how to get the backup filters
of ground coffee ready, so starting new coffee to brew is a two-
second affair rather than a minute and a half. After he has shown
me this and a number of other little tricks for staying ahead of the
game, he hangs around, skittish.

"Everything all right?" I ask.

"Mmmmph," he nods. He is looking around nervously, making
me feel like a girl he wants to ask to the prom. I go about my business, expecting him to leave at any second, but he doesn't. I'm
organizing the candy racks and he stands and watches me.

"What's up?" I ask.

"You friend a Tommy, right?"

"Yeah, I'm a friend of Tommy's."

"I need a favor." Apparently needing a favor necessitates that he speak clearly, because suddenly he can.

"What?"

"Tommy would get mad," he says, and stares at his shoes.

"How mad would Tommy get?"

"Labor cost. He's always talking about labor cost."

"What the hell are you talking about?"

"He hired you as an assistant manager, right?"

"Right."

Jughead nods wisely. "That means you get salary. You don't get overtime. He can work you ninety hours a week, and you get an average of whatever he promised you as an hourly wage. But I'm a minor. He's got to pay me overtime."

Well, I'll be damned. Tommy fucked me. I guess he had to. This is his job, and the corporate suits give him a bonus for no overtime. What am I going to do? Quit? Maybe I will after I've killed Corinne Gardocki. And perhaps a few others. "What's the favor, kiddo?"

"I want you to punch me out about a half hour after I've left." His face is guilt-ridden and red, and he stares at his shoes with shame as he relates this. "Tony, the guy who got shot, used to do it for me. We'd help each other out. But I gotta be somewhere on Sunday nights. That'll give me two hours of overtime, which is the minimum I need every two weeks to pay my dad a hundred dollars a week."

This poor kid. Where do they come from, people like this? A guy who is so ashamed to ask for a tiny break, who doesn't even expect it. He goes to high school full time, works a full-time job, and still doesn't feel he deserves a little extra so he can pay his dad rent money. "How about three hours overtime. Think that'll help?"

Jughead smiles, something I didn't believe possible. He turns to go.

"There's something you can do for me, though," I tell him as he is gathering his books from behind the counter. He studies sometimes when it is slow.

"Wozzat?" We're back to Jughead-ese now I'm asking the favor.
"Next Saturday night. I've got some shit I have to do. It'll take
about four hours, but Tommy's got me scheduled. I need you to
come in from about ten until two in the morning. Don't touch the
timecards, I'll just give you cash. Fifty bucks for four hours."

Jughead thinks. He's sharp enough not to ask questions. He
probably figures I'm running off to fuck someone's wife, rather than
kill her, an impression I'm going to foster by putting on cologne for
my Saturday night shift. "Fifty bucks?"

"Fifty big ones. Four easy hours."

"Deal."

"Deal." We nod at each other. He is gone.

The shift goes smoothly, but I notice something. Almost every customer fucks up the store somehow. Some put their nasty hands on
my freshly Windexed glass doors, some pick up things, examine the
price, then put them back in a different spot. Almost all of them
track dirt around on my mopped floor. I don't even want to talk
about the ones who ask for the key to the restroom.

This, I realize, is something that I have missed about working. I
actually have something to care about. I was good at managing the
loading dock, I checked invoices thoroughly, made sure every truck
going out had the correct items on it. In twelve years on the dock,
I got maybe half a dozen complaints from the receiving warehouses,
and a few of those I think somebody miscounted on the other end.
If something went missing in the warehouse, I'd spend hours trying
to locate it. If guys working the forklifts misplaced things, I'd make
sure they knew about it when it was discovered. And here, things
are no different. I want things in my workplace to be right.

Working for the man has nothing to do with it. If the head of the
Gas'n'Go empire called tomorrow and told me I was getting laid off
again, the quality of my work wouldn't suffer. I wouldn't stop
cleaning and start stealing, like they think I would, which is why,

if layoffs are ever necessary, you never find out until the last second. They consider every worker ant among them a potential felon, dying to get his hands on their stuff. But me and the guys I worked with weren't there for them, or even for our paychecks. We were there for ourselves, for the knowledge that we could work as a team and get things accomplished. And that was the worst part of getting laid off, the sudden realization that the team was a mirage, conjured up by management to get more work out of us for less pay. The things we accomplished meant nothing to anyone but us.

A guy comes in and looks at a candy bar. He spends three minutes looking at it, then throws it—throws it, not places it—back with the wrong candy bars. Then he comes to the counter.

"Hey man, you got any beef jerky?"

"Why?"

"What do you mean, why?" He is a skinny, shifty-looking guy, not young enough to be a kid but hardly a man. His thin face and the worn tattoos on his bony arms make me imagine he has a girlfriend who he beats. "'Cause I want to buy some."

"Are you sure?"

He stares at me.

"Are you sure," I continue, "that you don't want to just look at it and then throw it somewhere it doesn't belong?"

"Hey man, fuck you," he says, but is quick enough to back away toward the door as he says this. He sees me coming out from behind the counter and grabs a rack of sunglasses and pushes them toward me, scattering sunglasses all over the floor. He is gone before the last pair has come to a standstill.

I look up to see Jeff Zorda coming into the store, as I am down on my hands and knees gathering the sunglasses.

"Hey, Jake," Jeff laughs. "Tommy got you working here?" He points at the door. "What was up with that asshole?"

"He has no manners," I said. "I'm learning that most people don't."

Jeff steps over me on his way to the beer cooler. "You trying to teach him manners?"

"The lesson didn't go well."

Jeff shrugs, and plops a six-pack of imported beer on the counter. Imported. Things must be going well. Since the layoffs, Jeff has made do by involving himself in a number of scams, usually selling things over the Internet that he didn't have. He'd take the orders, cash the checks, then disappear. He was using the computers of people he knew were on vacation, or worse, in nursing homes. He'd scan the obituaries for the recently deceased, then do all kinds of things in their names.

"What line of work you in these days, Jeff?" I ring up the sale as he takes out his wallet.

"Need cable TV? I can hook you up. For you, half-price. Twenty-five dollars."

"I don't even have a TV anymore."

"I'll get you one of those, too."

"I'm all right. I'm getting used to reading."

Jeff looks at me, shakes his head. I'm a lost cause to him. He backs away from the counter in mock fear. "Don't teach me manners," he says, and laughs at his own wit. He leaves his palm print on the newly cleaned door on his way out.

A half hour later, the phone rings.

"Hello?"

"Jake?"

"Yeah?"

"I'm sending a guy in. With the gun. He'll be wearing a Packers jacket." Click and dial tone. About thirty seconds later, a guy wearing a Packers jacket comes in, doesn't look at me, heads straight to the beer cooler and gets a six-pack of imported. Imported. Everyone is doing well in this town but me. He strides to the counter, and pulls out his wallet. He is fortyish, with blond hair and a pockmarked face, his eyes blank and staring straight down as he hands me a twenty. I give him change, and he leaves without a word. And without giving me a gun.

Okay, so maybe that wasn't the guy. The Packers are popular around here. Then I see Ken Gardocki's SUV go driving slowly by, then take off along the boulevard. Then I remember Gas'n'Go's Fort Knox-like security system—God forbid someone should make off with a Tootsie roll—and I realize that the only place the cameras can't see is in the back corner, by the beer cooler. This guy was smart. I go back to the beer cooler and there is an object by the Budweiser, wrapped in an oily rag.

I crouch down on the floor and unwrap it. It is a shiny black pistol. I sit on the floor and stare at it for a while. I like the way that was done. That was teamwork.

The door opens and I stand up quickly to see my new customer, let him know there is someone in the store. It's the skinny beef jerky guy from earlier, only this time he's got two big friends. Really big. They are fat bastards, both over six foot five, and both look as dumb as rocks. He must have high-tailed back to the trailer park to find two morons he thought would intimidate me.

He strides toward me, the two dumbasses lumbering behind him. "Hey dipshit," he hisses, his voice full of hate. "You got any beef jerky?"

I stand up, the pistol held loosely in my hand where he can see it but the security cameras can't. I'd love to point it between his eyes, but that would ruin the teamwork. Keep away from the security cameras.

"No, but I've got a really nice pistol."

One of the dumbasses touches the skinny guy's shoulder.

"Man, he's got a gun," the dumbass says.

I look at the big guy. "Get the fuck outta here."

I turn back to the beer, as if I'm doing some kind of inventory. They leave quietly.

When I get home, I lay the gun out on the coffee table and stare at it with fascination. At this point, I should be thinking, this is a gun, a real gun I'm going to use to kill somebody, and the fact that

I have it in my apartment means there's no turning back. I'm not thinking that at all. I'm thinking about playing Cowboys and Indians when I was a kid.

That was the last time I held a gun, even a fake one. I've never had much use for guns. The only function a gun has is to kill people, and as I've never needed to do that before, I've had little experience. I can't recall ever shooting one as an adult, or even wanting to. I never had a desire to kill. I had a desire once to be a husband and a father and a breadwinner, not a killer. Oh well. In the immortal words of REO Speedwagon, ya gotta roll with the changes.

As for there being no turning back, there never was. I'm a man of my word. I said I'd do it and I will.

THREE

Tommy is working my ass off, and by Saturday I'm actually tired. Tired from work. What a beautiful, forgotten feeling that is. People who are having their asses worked off at their jobs don't appreciate what a gift that is, to feel that sense of satisfaction, the beauty of their exhaustion, which they can wear like a medal. It gives you energy, that exhaustion, knowing that you've contributed, made a difference. I made a difference by filling coffee pots and mopping floors and ringing up bags of potato chips and beer. I'm a worker again.

Tommy has me scheduled for every night this week and every night next week, all twelve-hour shifts. Even though I don't get overtime, I do get a management bonus for working over fifty hours a week, so he's trying to help me get back on my feet. I'm back on 'em, all right. My feet are starting to hurt. By the time Saturday afternoon rolls around, I'm washing my face in my ice-cold bathroom and I see my eyes in the mirror, surrounded by dark circles of exhaustion. That was the look I used to get at the factory before the spring started. Most businesses have their busy season just before Christmas. For us, it was when the winter ended, when farming got under way. We made machine-tooled parts for farm tractors, and sometimes in February and March we would work seventy and eighty hours a week. Those were the days of fat paychecks. When spring began, the men would all take their girlfriends and wives down to the car dealerships or furniture stores and trade in last year's model, or finally get that flat screen TV or sofa they had been talking about all winter. Now the car dealerships have moved, the furniture stores are boarded up, and I'm washing my exhausted face in cold water and toweling off before it turns to ice so I can get my ass to the convenience store and kill someone's adulterous stripper wife.

Saturday nights, I have learned, are never busy until the bars close. Then people come in and beg me to sell them beer after 2 a.m., which I have to be very firm about. The security cameras have timers on them, and if they film a beer transaction after two, it's big trouble for everybody. The local law enforcement agencies also send in underage kids and agents trying to buy beer illegally, so I have to card everyone and never sell the late beer, or I lose my job and Tommy does, too. Myself, I don't really give a fuck if they wanna get buzzed, but I don't want to cost Tommy his job, so I try to stick to the rules.

It strikes me as odd that these rules are being enforced now more than ever, even though the town has largely turned to trash. You'd think that things like this wouldn't matter so much, that we should all be left to fall apart in peace. But no. Rules are rules.

I bathe myself in cologne, remembering that Jughead expects me to be off committing adultery somewhere. I smell good. I grab my pistol, shove it down the back of my pants under my jacket, and I'm off for my shift at the Gas'n'Go.

* * *

The evening is uneventful, and at ten o'clock sharp, Jughead comes in to relieve me for four hours. I'm to be back at 2 a.m. I need to be back then, because that's the time the alcohol law enforcement folks might stop by and try to buy illegal beer, and they might notice an underage worker behind the counter.

Before I go, I adjust the time on the surveillance system to read last night. Now, the tapes will show FRI on them instead of SAT. Then I'll do the same thing for every night this week. If I ever become a suspect, the police will have to look back through six nights of surveillance tapes to prove I wasn't in the store when Corinne Gardocki got shot, and I'll just claim the surveillance system is a piece of shit that can't keep time. I can't see why I'd ever be a suspect, but you can't be too careful.

When Jughead comes in, I've already stuffed my pockets with rags from the cleaning closet I can use to wrap around my boots so I don't leave bootprints in the snow. I think that's all the preparation I'll need. At 10:01, I wave goodbye to Jughead, who is opening his schoolbooks and starting to study at the counter, and I'm on my way to make Corinne Gardocki dead.

I'm walking the whole way. It's a little over five miles out to the Gardocki place, and the average person walks three miles an hour, so I should have about a half hour to get the job done before I have to turn and walk back. I've decided my car is too much of a risk. What if I have a fender bender on the ice pulling out of the Gardocki driveway? What if I break down half a mile from the murder scene? How do I explain my presence there? Besides, I've driven to work tonight, and made sure my car is parked in front of the outdoor security camera.

A light snow is falling and the cars drive by me as I make my way along the darkened streets, their tires hissing on the pavement. It is a busy Saturday night on the roads, but not as busy as it used to be. The town has depopulated a good bit since the layoffs, and a lot of people just stay home nowadays and stare at the walls, which is all they can afford to do. Until I got my convenience store job, that was what I did. Stare at the walls and try to go to sleep early. I pass a small corner bar, and through the faded yellow window I see two old men inside, pissing away their social security or veteran's benefits for a chance to die somewhere other than their one-bedroom apartments. The snow turns to a hard drizzle, and I start thinking about getting out of this town. What's Florida like this time of year?

I turn off the road and cross a field, walk through the empty lots of an old industrial park, cross disused train tracks. I go through broken fences and across an unused access road, everything a reminder of a civilization that used to be and is no more. Gutted, the whole town. Empty buildings, rusted vehicles, broken and disused equipment lying everywhere. This town reminds me of old photos I saw in school of World War II battlefields, with blown-apart tanks and overturned jeeps lying all around, the only difference being that the dead bodies which lay everywhere in the pictures are the still-living zombies populating the town.

Why don't I leave? Why don't I just take my next paycheck and hop a train to Florida and be done with it? Because I was born here. I wanted to live here my whole life. Like most of the people here, I was happy with the place, liked surviving the winters, loved the first coming of spring. I wanted to take my kids down to Lake Michigan in the summertime. I wanted Ernie Enright, the best, most honest mechanic I've ever known, to fix my car. I imagined growing old, and still being able to drive to the Packers games from my home near the lake, which I had bought with savings and investments and my 401k which had taken me a lifetime to accumulate. I lived within ten miles of where I was born, within ten miles of where Kelly was born, and I liked it that way.

I pass the factory. It is surrounded by a ten-foot-high fence, topped with razor wire. Someone is worried that people will steal tractor-building equipment and start making tractors in their basements. A huge sign above the entrance announces that the land is for lease. I hear Ken Gardocki's words: The factory days here are over. I look at the lease sign and realize how right he is. Who the hell would lease this place? Is a competing tractor-parts firm going to snap at the opportunity to reopen the gates of a rusted factory which other executives already decided, for whatever reason, wasn't profitable enough? Our stock was going up when they closed the plant, just not fast enough. It could be improved upon. So improve it they did.

A mile farther on, I come to the bridge over Kruc Creek, where I'm supposed to throw the gun on my way back, after the job is done. I look down into the water, which is a real torrent tonight, what with all the rain and sleet. Good plan. The gun will get washed into the mud and buried forever. I walk quickly across the bridge. I'm getting soaked through, but I don't really mind that much. The cold feels good. I'll have some coffee when I get back to the store. Corinne Gardocki, who is alive now, will be dead then, when I have my next cup of coffee. She's probably getting fucked by an airline pilot right now, with no idea how close death is.

About a half-mile from the bridge, I cut back through some trees, the final leg of my journey. The shortcut will bring me around the back of the Gardocki place. So as not to leave boot prints, I wrap the towels tightly around my feet. I take out the gun, check it, take off the safety. I pull my hood up and walk up to the edge of the treeline facing the Gardocki's back yard. There is a light on in the kitchen and through the kitchen door I can see Corinne puttering around in lingerie.

I can feel my heart pounding as I drop into a crouch and dart quickly up against the side of the house, the snow making an awful crunching noise with every step. I can't believe everyone in town can't hear this, because it's so goddamned quiet except for my heart pounding and my feet making shotgun-blast steps in the snow, and except for the low growls coming out of the huge kennel which, until now, I haven't even noticed is sitting at the end of the driveway.

A dog. Christ. Ken Gardocki has a dog. And it's big and it's coming right at me, fast. It is a blur of anger and growls and fur, flying across the twenty yards that separate us, too intent on the idea of tearing my throat out to emit any sound but a furious growl as it closes the distance in what must be a half second, which is just one microsecond more than I need to level the gun right at its head and squeeze the trigger.

BANG.

The gun kicks. The noise is godawful. My ears are ringing. The dog slides to a stop at the bottom of the steps leading up to the kitchen and lies there, upside down. He twitches once and is still. I lean back against the side of the house, and I hear myself softly repeating "shit shit shit" over and over, like a mantra. Then the door opens.

Corinne Gardocki sticks her head out and I shoot her.

BANG.

She pitches forward and falls down the steps onto her dog, her head sliding under the dog's belly. In her negligee, the scene looks bizarre, her head buried in the dog's genitalia.

The echo of the gunshot dies and it is completely quiet. The snow is falling on both bodies, and I sit and stare at them for a full minute, lit up by the slim light from the kitchen, letting the ringing in my ears subside. Far off I can hear a car driving by, driven by someone who has no idea what has transpired here at the Gardocki household, unaware that less than half a mile from him or her, two beings, alive two minutes ago, are now dead in a pile.

The shots must have been audible for ten miles, I imagine. I think of Jughead, back at the convenience store, looking up from his books, wondering what those gunshots were. Then I realize that if a neighbor heard them, he would probably be dialing an emergency number right now. I push myself away from the wall of the house, take a last look at the scene, and dash off through the snow, through the trees, back onto the roadway. I tuck the gun back into my jeans, and take the two rags off my feet and throw them over the bridge into Kruc Creek.

The gun I keep. I can't bear the thought of tossing it. The gun and I are connected now. I'll take my chances.

My ears are still ringing. One thing I've learned . . . I need a silencer. That loud banging noise every time I pull the trigger just won't do.

I get back to the store with fifteen minutes to spare, soaking and frozen through. Jughead looks up when I come in.

"Wanneystay tutoo?" Do I want him to stay until two?

"Nah, thanks. I appreciate it." I take two twenties and a ten out of my pocket, where they have soaked through, and I hand him the dripping money.

He nods wordlessly, grabs his books and is gone. He couldn't care less where I have been. He could never be a witness against me anyway. He'd give a court stenographer fits. "Where was Mr. Skowran the night of the killing?" "Hebelyt he fawar reeg."

I sit down and make a cup of coffee, and stare into space. By the time Tommy comes in, at seven in the morning, my hair has dried, my jacket is merely damp, and I'm ready to go home to a satisfying sleep.

The killing was so easy, so fast, that I can't believe I'm getting my gambling debt wiped out and eight hundred dollars just for that. It was nothing. I shot the dog out of instinct, and Corinne too. The situation just developed, and I reacted with an efficiency I had forgotten existed in myself. When you're out of work, it becomes difficult to evaluate yourself because you're never in stressful situations. Well, that was stressful, and I did good.

Why would someone who heard a gunshot in her backyard come outside on a snowy, dark night wearing nothing but a negligee? What were her final thoughts? I wonder this as I watch my breath evaporate in the frigid air of my apartment. She didn't even know I was hiding against the house, the first inkling she had was the bullet entering her head. I did everything wrong, yet everything turned out right.

I know what to do now. Nothing. All the things I've heard about murderers, that they love to sign their work with some kind of personal touch, that they compulsively return to the scene of the crime, that they brag about their killings to friends, cut out newspaper articles about their crime and save them all over their apartments, I won't do any of that. I won't call Ken Gardocki, either. I'll let him contact me.

I hide the gun in my closet. This might be the dumbest thing I've ever done, keeping the gun. It is the only thing that connects me to the murder, and the minute it is gone, I'm safe. But I want it. I consider it an instrument of work, and work is a thing of honor. That's something that the people who closed the factory never understood.

FOUR

Monday morning, 5 a.m. The newspaper guy brings the papers, dumps them out front of the store in a bundle and drives off. I eagerly go out and cut the string, put the newspapers in the rack, then take one out to see if my crime has shocked the city.

Nothing. Not on the front page, anyway. There's a lot of stuff about a local hospital closing its doors because no one can pay their bills anymore, and some Washington pol got caught doing something bad with funds earmarked for some great cause. Never heard of him. I flip back to page two. Nothing. Trouble in the Congo and the Middle East. Isn't there always? I toss the whole section and grab the thinner "Town and Area" section, which holds the comics. Nothing on the front page of the section, just more about the hospital. After flipping past eight pages of friggin' hospital articles, which I guess are supposed to make me feel something (What the

41

fuck were they expecting? That the hospital managers would just keep helping sick people out of the goodness of their hearts? We know by now that nobody gives a fuck about us, so we don't care about this shit, just give us a paper full of comics and sports and shut the fuck up with this manipulative liberal ass-kissing that's supposed to make me feel sorry for myself), I see a small article on the bottom corner of page nine which is headlined WOMAN, DOG, SHOT BY INTRUDER. In the article, which is three short paragraphs, one paragraph less than was devoted to the trouble in the Congo, I learn that a neighbor found Corinne Gardocki, 39, Sunday morning when he noticed her body lying on the back steps.

She was thirty-nine? Bet she wouldn't have wanted the whole town to know that. I thought she was a good bit younger. Police Sergeant Somebody-or-Other was ruling it a homicide, tipped off, I suppose, by the gunshot wound in the head. He surmised that a Peeping Tom (I beg your pardon!) had been watching Mrs. Gardocki when the family dog attacked, and violence had begun.

I get my first criminal impulse, an insane desire to call this cop and set him straight, tell him I'm not a Peeping Tom, I'm a respectable assassin, thank you very much. Of course, I overcome the impulse, but I feel slightly offended. I also have a strong desire to go back there, look around, see how the place looks in daylight without a dead woman and dog on the back steps, see the yellow police tape around the place, tape for which I am solely responsible. There is most likely a cop sitting out front, waiting for the criminal to return to the scene of the crime, as they almost always do, supposedly. Now I see why. I'm surprised at how strong the urge is.

I fold up the newspaper and put it back in the rack.

Tommy comes in at seven. We chat for a bit. He tells me that his wife, Mel, got a job for an insurance company, administrative assistant. I congratulate him.

"We might even be able to pay all our bills this month," he tells me.

As I'm walking out the door, he asks, "Jake, man, have you been fucking with the security system? All the tapes say Friday."

"Haven't touched it. I don't do well with technology."

He shrugs. "Maybe it was Jughead."

I shrug. "See you tonight."

"Later."

So the only suspicious thing I've done is screw with the security system. Someone has noticed. What to do now? Screw with it more, or leave it alone? I figure just take the tape and throw it out might be the best thing. Or tape over it. We're supposed to keep the tapes in order, each one lasts twenty-four hours, and there are fourteen, so we can go back two weeks. If I mix up the order, and throw the incriminating tape in tonight, I won't need to worry about it anymore.

And I can't control the urge to walk up past the Gardocki place again. Instead of driving home, I drive about a mile away from the Gardocki residence, park on a quiet street, and walk around. I want to walk past the house, to see if there really is a cop car outside. Maybe they've set up a surveillance camera to see who walks by. I get to the bridge over Kruc Creek and see not one, but four cop cars, and a police van, parked next to the bridge.

"Morning," I say to one of the cops. He is standing by his car, drinking coffee from a paper cup. He nods. Down in the creek I see two other cops, dressed in hip boots, splashing around.

"Somebody drown?" I ask.

"Nah," says the cop. "Just looking for some stuff."

I don't say anything, am about to continue walking, when the cop, out of boredom, volunteers some information. "There was a homicide up the road over the weekend. We got a tip that a guy driving by saw someone throwing something into the creek, about the time of the murder."

I look awed, impressed by the importance of police work. "Wow," I say.

The cop looks pleased with my reaction. This guy isn't wondering about me, he's thinking about himself, about impressing an

average joe with the details of his job. I could impress him might-
ily by telling him I'm the guy they're looking for, but I'm prudent
enough to just smile and nod.

"Have a good day," I tell him, walking off.

"You too," he says, Clint Eastwood-like.

So it seems my decision not to throw the gun in the creek was
a good one after all. Someone up there, maybe the patron saint of
hired killers, is looking out for me. About time.

"There's going to be some kind of review," Tommy tells me the next
morning as I am preparing to hand him the reins of the business.
"Some guy will be coming down from the head office, going over
stuff, checking out the store. I think he rates the employees. You're
going to have to talk to him."

"When?"

"Today. They just called."

"Sounds like fun."

Tommy nods. He has stress circles around his eyes that he used
to get during the beginning of farm season back at the factory. He's
a good guy, always trying, always working to make his life and the
lives of his family better, always getting fucked by circumstance and
making the best of it. He nearly lost his house when the layoffs
came, but he called the bank and worked things out. Every now and
then I hear rumors about his wife and some other guy from the factory, but she and Tommy are still together. He works it out. Now
he's trying to work out the inventory list. He has a look of fear about
him, anticipating some kind of criticism from the corporate types
who are on their way, doing everything in his power to prevent it.

The store makes money, but since the layoffs I've learned that's
hardly the point. Making money is neither here nor there. What
matters is, are you making as much money as is humanly possible,
and if not, why not. And the people who determine the limits of
human possibility with regards to money-making, using totally

theoretical ideas they've dreamed up over glasses of wine or late-night poker games, will determine whether Tommy is doing a good job solely on the criteria of their imaginary profit margins. So the fact that Tommy works over seventy hours a week, cleaning, counting, ordering, worrying, means nothing. If there isn't a large enough display from the most profitable soda company visible from the street, and the profits are not being maximized, then Tommy has to be criticized, even punished, in the form of a bad review.

"Anything I can do to help?"

Tommy looks at me, his eyes wide with worry. "Just make sure everything is clean. In the back."

"It is, man. I cleaned everything last night."

"I need you to hang out for a while," he says. "You have to talk to this guy. He wants to meet all the employees."

"No problem."

He walks around muttering to himself, shifting boxes, moving milk around so all the labels face out. There are all kinds of rules.

"Is the door to the security room locked?"

"No, it never is."

"Don't tell the guy that," Tommy says, alarmed. "Tell him it's always locked."

"Okay." The security room, where we keep the surveillance tapes, doubles as a break room, so if we locked it, we'd never be able to take breaks. When it's slow at night, I go back there, eat a microwaveable sandwich, read the paper, sit down for a bit, away from the security cameras and the fluorescent lights. This is against the rules? I realize suddenly that tearing their pamphlet into dust without reading to page three might have created trouble for Tommy. I have to learn answers to anticipated questions.

"Is there anything else I should say?" I ask.

Tommy shrugs, even smiles. "Just be honest."

"Always."

* * *

The guy comes in at ten o'clock, an hour late, which means an hour of extra standing around for me. The first thing he says when he walks in the door is, "The *USA Today* box is in the wrong position. It should be to the right of the *Courier*." He ignores me as I stand behind the counter, and shakes Tommy's hand without smiling, looking around the store as he does this. He is a young man, maybe thirty, in a nice gray suit, hair immaculate, clean shaven. He has a critical eye, designed to inspire insecurity in anyone he meets, and my first thought upon seeing him is, do I look presentable? Did I shave last night? Am I as presentable as the models on the pamphlet cover? I stroke my chin. Stubble.

He looks at me as he and Tommy head toward the back. He has a frozen, unfriendly smile as he asks me, "Don't we wear smocks here?"

As long as I've worked here, I've never even seen one of the brown Gas'n'Go smocks the employees wear on the pamphlet cover.

"I'll get him one," Tommy says quickly. He disappears into the back and comes out a few seconds later with a brown smock, which he hands to me. "Here, Jake," he says, giving me the smock as if we've both been looking for it everywhere.

"Just try to make sure they're wearing those smocks," the corporate guy says cheerfully, as if it doesn't matter, but letting us know that he really thinks it's the most important thing in the world. Tommy nods vigorously and starts making an excuse but the guy hushes him, the issue is closed, nothing more needs to be said about the smock. They go into the back. I go outside and switch the *USA Today* and *Courier* boxes.

Then, for an hour and a half I stand there, waiting on customers, wondering if these two are ever coming out, wondering when this silliness will be over and I can go home and get some sleep. It is well past noon when they come out of the meeting, and Tommy looks much the same as he did when he went in, stressed, tormented.

"Jake," Tommy says, "Mr.Brecht wants to meet with you now." He looks worried that I'm going to spill some kinds of beans, unwittingly get Tommy in trouble. Tommy tries to make eye contact with me as I go back, as if to clarify that we share a bond, that I'm on his side. Of course I am. Why does he feel like this? Why does the corporate guy want him to feel like this? Do nervousness and fear make one a more loyal employee? I go into the cramped little back room, where the corporate guy is sitting behind Tommy's desk, which he has actually moved away from the wall so the desk separates us, clarifying the relationship.

"Mr. Skowran," he says, reviewing my employee file, which can't be very thick. It contains two pieces of paper, a W-2 and an application form, on which I wrote my name and my phone number at Tommy's request. I've worked here just over a week and have yet to receive a paycheck. What's to review?

"What we're doing here is a periodic review of store management," he tells me. I had forgotten until now that I am listed on the employee payroll as an assistant manager. "But we've been particularly concerned about Eight One Eight."

"About what?"

"Eight One Eight." He looks at me, folds his hands on the desk.

Okay, I give up. "What's Eight One Eight?"

"It's this store," he says, incredulous at my ignorance. "Gas'n'Go unit Eight One Eight."

"Oh," I say. "The store."

"Yes. The store."

"Why are you concerned about it?" I'm a full-time employee, and I'm not concerned one bit. What's so concerning about a little gas station that sells beer and soda and makes a profit?

"We came down here," he says, "because of the trouble you had last week." Did I have trouble last week? I try to recall. Then I realize he must be talking about the kid getting shot by cops while selling drugs out of the store. "Gas'n'Go's name appeared in a number of news reports about the incident. We can't have that."

I nod.

He looks at me piercingly, trying to make me uneasy, while I imagine how he would die if I shot him. I wonder if this man has ever loved anyone. I doubt it. Has he ever been really angry about anything? I doubt that, too. The range of emotions available to him are limited due to his obsession with greed and his belief in its rewards. I imagine he did fairly well in college, and at some point in his personal development he learned that ruthlessness was rewarded with money. Maybe he had a summer job once with a man who cared about nothing but money and made lots of it, and he listened to everything this man said, even quoted it to himself while he drove back and forth to work. He probably uses those quotes still. They were quotes like "Hard work is the only thing that pays the bills," and he confuses hard work with aggressively acquiring money, and believes himself a worker in the most basic sense. Humor, passion, love and art are distractions. This is the type of man who ran the company that laid us all off. He finally asks me, "Mr. Skowran, do you use drugs?"

"Can't afford 'em," I tell him jovially, in an effort to bring some level of humanity into the conversation. He doesn't smile back.

"What we need from you, is a urine sample," he says. He looks at me as if this news is supposed to shock me to my boots. He thinks this conversation, to me, is a fight for my job, and my life. In fact, it is he who is interviewing for his life. I've got a gun at home and I've just discovered that I like to use it, and if he insults me unnecessarily, he is going to be the first of what I am planning will be a number of people who will pay with their lives for what has been done to my town. I don't like him, or his attitude, and somebody is going to pay and it is going to be somebody with an attitude just like his. Telling Tommy to move the newspaper boxes around before you have even introduced yourself, is that a reason to die? Hell, yes. It really is. Whatever happened to civility? But it's not just that. It's this attempt to inspire fear, to be the alpha male. What has he ever done that he should be in charge of two grown

men like Tommy and myself, except demonstrate an ability to
behave with murderous money-hunger for a company with a sim-
ilar mindset?

But I have to proceed carefully because I don't want to get
Tommy in trouble. So, to his revelation that he wants a urine sample, I stifle the urge to ask him if he'd like it right now, in his face,
and I nod peacefully.

"We're drug testing all our employees," he explains.

I nod.

"I'll give you a chit, and you have to go by the clinic later today
and give them a sample. The chit has the directions on it."

I nod again.

"And I'll be around for the next few days," he tells me. "Just to
make sure things run right."

I nod. "Excellent."

My appointment at the clinic is at two in the afternoon, which, as
I work nights, is like scheduling someone for an appointment at
two in the morning. I have to be at work at seven, because, with
this corporate fuckstick around, we can't let Jughead work at night
due to the minor laws. The result is that I'm not getting any sleep
for nearly forty-eight hours.

I show up to see what is probably the busiest workplace in this
town. Secretaries, receptionists, women in white smocks, all running around with clipboards and vials of pee. It's good to know
someone is making money around here. The girl behind the desk
takes my chit and tells me to have a seat. I have barely sat down
when another woman comes up. The place seems to be staffed
entirely by females, making it the prime pick-up location in town,
now that most of the bars have gone.

"Mr. Skowran?" she says, her voice hard and official.

"Yes?"

"Do you have your chit?"

I hand her the paper and she hands me a plastic vial. "Fill this up to the line. Use Bathroom One."

She walks off, a bundle of efficiency. I go into the bathroom with a big "One" on the door, quickly fill the vial, screw that cap on, wipe my piss off the outside, then notice that washing my hands is impossible because the water has been shut off. I assume this is so we can't add water to our urine to make our drug use less detectable. I go outside, holding a clear vial of my urine, wondering who to hand it to. The woman who gave me the vial is gone, and everyone else looks busy. A woman walks by with a clipboard and I ask her who gets the sample, and she says, "Heather" and keeps walking. I stand there for a few minutes more, holding my piss in my hand. I haven't slept in thirty-six hours and I'm being drug tested for a six-fifty-an-hour job which leaves me too broke to buy drugs. What if I was using drugs? Would a horrific drug-addled mistake by a convenience store clerk really endanger society, if I put an extra bag of coffee in the coffee machine, or misplaced the beef jerky display? Heaven forbid I should forget to wear my smock. I put the full vial of urine down on the receptionist's desk and say, "Here you go. Bye."

She backs away from the urine vial as if it were a live snake and starts calling after me, but I'm already out the door. A furious woman in a white smock comes out into the parking lot. "You can't just do that," she tells me. "You have to wait for—"

"Fuck you."

I'm in my car and gone, and as I'm pulling out of the parking lot I see this woman copying my license plate. Is she going to call the cops? Am I to be charged with leaving piss unattended? Something fundamental about my tolerance for bullshit, and my ability to relate to others, has changed since I blew Corinne Gardocki's brains out. The rules by which I have lived my entire life, rules of conduct, are disintegrating before my eyes. I see them for what they are, a carefully designed system to keep me in line, to keep me from asking for more, like Oliver Twist. Now that I have stepped out of line in the worst way, there's really no reason to stay in line in all the smaller ways. If that woman makes any trouble for me, I'll blow her fucking brains all over the street. Drug test this, you bitch. I'm going home to get some sleep. Go ahead, call the store, tell that corporate guy on me. I don't much care for that guy. He'll be dead in two days anyway.

Just as I am pulling the sheets up over my head, there is a knock on the door.

Oh, Christ, who could that be? Has Financially Consolidated Finances, or whatever the hell they're called, finally started making house calls? Have the cops tracked me down for the piss incident? I get out of bed, grumbling furiously, and open the door to see the pockmarked face of the guy who gave me the gun in the convenience store, still wearing the Packers jacket. Ken Gardocki's henchman.

"Ken wants to talk to you," he says.

"When?"

"How's now?"

"I haven't slept in days."

"He's got money for you."

"Let's go."

He comes inside and watches me closely as I pull on my jacket. Is he checking me for a wire?

It has started to snow again. I go downstairs and hop in Ken Gardocki's SUV, which has the heat on full blast and a Kenny G CD blaring from the flawless speakers. It is like being in another world, enclosed, safe, a wall against the elements provided by money. I want this, the SUV, the speakers, the contoured bucket seats, even the damned Kenny G CD. This was what I had before the closings, what I had earned. Nothing against my 21-year-old Honda Civic, but the windows don't roll up and the radio doesn't work and I realize, as I relax in the bucket seat and we pull out onto the main road, that it's hard to go backwards. Once you've had something, you always believe you deserve it.

"Is this a Cherokee?" I ask the pockmarked guy.

"*Grand* Cherokee." He stares out the window blankly, concentrating on driving in the worsening weather. Who is this fellow? I've never seen him around town. If he's such a right-hand man to Gardocki, why doesn't *he* kill people for him?

"What's your name?" I ask.

He continues driving. He is looking for a road sign. He doesn't know the area that well, not being from around here.

"Is this Exit 31?" he asks. About three seconds ago we passed a huge highway sign saying "Exit 31." No-name Pockmarked Guy isn't the swiftest caribou in the herd. I don't feel like dealing with any more of his silent routine, so I decide to badger him until he starts talking.

"Yes, it is," I tell him as he wrenches the wheel, taking us over two lanes, barely making the exit without hitting a concrete barrier. "I asked you what your name was."

"What's it to you?"

"All right then. Where are we going?"

"You'll see."

There's something about this guy I don't get. It's like he's playing the part of Ken Gardocki's henchman, based on years of TV watching. He learned how a henchman should act by watching *The Rockford Files*. Why doesn't he just talk to me?

I start noticing we are going down roads increasingly more remote, getting out into the country. Trees have replaced buildings. This would be an excellent place to dump a body, say, the body of someone who has just committed a murder for you and you want to shut them up for good. I wonder if there is a freshly dug grave around here, waiting for me. But then, if this idiot was going to kill me, why didn't he just kill Corinne Gardocki and he and Ken could have left me out of it? I watch Pockmark carefully, wondering if he has a gun. If he does, I'll be ready. I'll wrestle it from him and put a few rounds in his ugly dumbass skull before he has a chance to . . . .

"This is it," he says, as he pulls into the gravel parking lot of a small bar, hard to notice even from the road, covered on all sides by thick, snow-covered trees. There are a few pickup trucks in the parking lot, getting dusted by the snow. The bar has neon beer signs out front, but apparently no name.

He parks, shuts the car off and gets out wordlessly. He starts walking toward the bar, then realizes I am still in the car. "You coming?" He walks inside.

What's wrong with this asshole? Aren't henchmen supposed to have manners, to get the door for me? I get out of the car and trot over to the entrance just as he slams the bar door in my face.

Inside, the bar is better lit and more lively than I imagined. Ken Gardocki is shooting pool with some older guys I remember from the factory, and they nod to me as I walk up to the table.

"Jake!" Ken smiles and shakes my hand with a warmth and exuberance I hadn't expected. "Good to see you." He starts leading me over to a booth, and Pockmark looks like he is coming with us. Gardocki turns to Pockmark. "Hey Karl, why don't you shoot in my place while I chat with my friend Jake here." Karl. So that's his name. He looks disappointed about not joining us, but he goes over to the pool table and grabs a cue, eyeing us as we sit down.

"Fuck's the matter with that guy?" I ask.

"Who, Karl?" Gardocki laughs. "He's all right. Not too smart. I have him run errands for me, but nothing too serious."

"Where did you meet him? I haven't seen him around before."

Gardocki doesn't want to talk about Karl. He takes a pay packet out of his shirt pocket and gives it to me. "You did good," he says.

"Thanks." For the first time in months, my work has been appreciated. Gardocki is looking at me with the intense gaze I remember from our first meeting. "Are you interested in more?"

"More what?" It takes me a second. "More work? Of this nature?"

Gardocki says nothing.

"Yeah, I guess so." I think about it for a second. So there is work to be found in this town after all. I am being offered more work, how cool is that? "Same pay?"

"We'll see if we can't get you a raise. This one might involve some travel."

"Travel?"

"Ever been to New York City?"

Wow. This is too good to be true. A free vacation. I could sure use one. "I've never been there."

"How's next week? Can you get off at the convenience store?"

"Sure." I'm getting used to his habit of casually letting me know he is aware of every detail of my life.

"This one might be tricky," he tells me.

"I love a challenge."

Gardocki grins. "Take off from work Thursday and Friday. I'll take care of all the arrangements. I'll get $2,500 to you as a startup fee, probably give you another five Gs after the fact. This isn't for me," he adds. "It's for a friend, in New York. We switch off doing favors for each other."

"Cool."

"So I can count on you?"

"Absolutely."

We shake hands. "I'll have Karl drive you home."

Gardocki goes back over to the pool table and talks to Karl. Karl looks over at me, then walks out to the car. I'm supposed to follow. The door slams in my face again as we go outside.

I get to sleep for an hour before being back at the convenience store to relieve Jughead at seven. Jughead is wearing a brown Gas'n'Go smock, which means our corporate friend must still be around. Jughead is not doing his homework at the counter, as usual, but is staring straight ahead like a Buckingham Palace guard.

I go up to the counter, and I see a corporate ID card near the register. James Brecht. He's never bothered to introduce himself.

Jughead doesn't acknowledge me when I walk in, which means Brecht must have talked to him about excessive speech, or some such thing. Perhaps talking to other employees is discouraged in the manual. But the manual got pulverized. No matter, Brecht greets me with another one as I walk back into the surveillance room/office to hang up my coat. And put on the smock which is in his other hand.

"Hi, Jim," he says as he walks past me with a clipboard and motions for me to follow him. He taps his watch and shows it to me. Seven-oh-six. "Let's try to get here on time, okay? We've got a lot to do tonight." He walks me up to the rack of potato chips and dip, one of our big sellers. "All Wenke products have to be on the top shelf, okay? I need you to go through the whole store and get Wenke products on the top shelves. Vienna sausages, potato chips, whatever. We've got to get them into view." He looks briefly irritated, then adds, "We've been sending Tommy memos about this for weeks, but nothing got done."

"Wenke on top shelf," I say, pulling on the smock. "Check."

"I'm going to be the day manager here for a while," he says.

"What's happened to Tommy?"

"He'll be joining you behind the counter until he's proved he can handle the pressure of running this store." Brecht doesn't want to part with any more details, and starts reciting more things to do with stock.

"You demoted Tommy? To clerk?"

Brecht doesn't want to talk about this. "We came to an understanding," he says, showing me both palms, the gesture of friendliness and peace which is supposed to mollify the angry. I'm not angry, I'm just curious and concerned for Tommy, and the gesture annoys me. I pretend to listen to him as he walks around and describes things to do, and I wonder when he will go home.

"Kenneth?" Brecht calls over to Jughead, who is still staring straight ahead.

"Yes?" Jughead screams.

"Jim's here, you can clock out now."

"It's Jake."

He looks at me for a moment, as if absorbing this information into the deepest recesses of his brain. His eyes assure me he will never make that mistake again. He never will. "Jake," he says.

Jughead walks out wordlessly, and Brecht says, in a low, conversational voice, "Did you ever notice that kid is hard to understand?"

I shake my head.

Brecht shrugs and continues walking me down the aisles. "Oh," he says off-handedly as he moves a bag of Wenke chips from foot level to the top. "Was there a problem at the drug-testing center?"

"No, no problem. There was a long wait. I needed to—"

"I'm going to need that clean drug test."

"You're going to get it."

Two and half hours later, Brecht is still here. He is back in the office. I have already done most of the things I was expected to do tonight and would be smoking out front, if there was no chance he would catch me and give me a five-minute patronizing lecture about it, when he calls me into the back room. It is dark in there, but for a small black and white TV he has brought in. He has been watching videos from the surveillance cameras from the past week, like a football coach going over game tape. I expect he has drawn up a chalkboard somewhere with x's and o's, game plans for how we can better serve the customer.

"Jake, we've got a problem," he tells me.

Oh, Christ. He's noticed I've played with the camera dates. He knows I've had Jughead work for me late-night. He knows, he knows, he knows. He knows everything.

"I've been watching videos from the past week."

"Yeah?"

He hits play, and there is a picture of me, behind the counter. I can't read the date and time on the video. "Are you seeing what I'm seeing?"

"Me behind a counter?"

Brecht takes off his glasses. "Jake, I've watched all the videos from last week." He looks at me, so earnest, and in his eyes I see all the knowledge of all my crimes. He has pieced it together somehow, the altered surveillance, the newspaper articles of the murder, everything. "In all those videos from last week, I don't see a single employee wearing a smock."

Wearing a what? That's what this guy has been back here doing? In my relief, I offer information. "We weren't wearing smocks until you showed up," I tell him.

"Tommy told me you were," he says, shaking his head.

Oh, Christ, what have I done now? I've gotten Tommy into trouble while trying to get myself out. He sees me still standing in the doorway. "Thanks Jake. Just get back to the front."

Brecht finally leaves at two in the morning. While he is leaving, he puts his jacket on the counter to go back into the office to get something he has forgotten. I reach into the jacket pocket and pull out a hotel entrance card, Kellner Suites. I know where that is, about two miles away, up Route 40. I drop the card back into his pocket as he comes out of the office.

As soon as he is gone, I fall asleep. We don't get another customer until after Tommy comes in at seven. Or maybe we did, and I just slept through it. I guess we'll find out when we look at the video.

FIVE

I get back to the store for my night shift at 7 p.m., and Tommy is waiting for me with my first paycheck from Gas'n'Go.

Four hundred and eighteen dollars, after taxes. That doesn't seem like much for two weeks of non-stop work, but it'll get my TV back from the pawnshop. Added to the eight hundred I've received from Ken Gardocki, I can now pay rent, turn my heat back on, maybe even look into a cheap cable package.

And things get better. Tommy, who has been demoted to clerk until he gets his shit together and learns how to run a Gas'n'Go right, needs to hire someone else for the overnight shift. Brecht has told him that I'm working too much, and becoming cranky. Brecht doesn't know the half of it. Tommy had massively overscheduled me to do me a favor, because he knew I was broke. This idea has been nixed by Brecht. I'm not performing my customer service adequately, I'm told, and I am offered a few days off. This is

59

perfect, as it allows me to go to New York to kill someone over the weekend.

"You can have tonight off," Tommy tells me. This is fine with me, I'm exhausted. Then he adds, "Come back Monday night."

Which is also perfect. I've got the days off I need without asking for them. But something funny is going on here. "Am I being suspended?"

"It's not a suspension, Jake, you need a rest—"

"Fuck that guy."

"Jake, come on. I need this job. I've got Mel and Jenny to worry about. This is all there is right now. You know what things are like. Besides, you *do* need a rest. Look at you. You slept most of last night. Brecht saw the video."

"Fucking video. Jesus Christ, we're being watched on a video. Doesn't that piss you off? Seven bucks an hour and they're watching us on videos? What are we, lab rats?"

Tommy is just staring at me. I sigh. Maybe he's right. I've got over a thousand dollars now and I haven't had a beer in weeks. I take my paycheck and turn to go. "Monday, I'll be back, right? I'll still have a job?"

Tommy nods eagerly, glad that I'm leaving without more of a fuss. "Monday. I promise."

I go down to Tulley's for a beer.

Like everything else in town, Tulley's has a has-been quality to it. It is a dive bar about a mile from the factory entrance, which was packed every night up until the layoffs, but now it just looks like a bar with way too much space. The fifty-car parking lot never has more than three or four beat-up wrecks in it.

I stopped going in for a while after the layoffs, not because I had no money, but because I couldn't stand the emptiness of it. It was the saddest reminder of what had happened to us. Each barstool and booth had a memory for me. This is where Tommy met Mel, that one is where I met Kelly. Those barstools are where Tommy, Jeff Zorda and I used to sit on Sundays and watch the Packers. Now all the booths were empty, and their emptiness revealed a truth about them. They were shoddy. The bar was shoddy, the woodwork was crap. There was really nothing attractive about any of it, except the idea that people had enjoyed themselves here for years.

"Jake? Haven't seen you around here much lately. What you been up to?"

Big Tony Wolek is the bartender and manager, a worn, three-hundred pound drinker who took a massive pay cut when the factory closed. To make back the money he lost, he now has to work all day, every day, and he looks about done. He wheezes as he brings me my Budweiser with a glass. I haven't been here in months, but he remembers my beer and how I like it. As he puts it down in front of me, I think, this man is going to die soon. His skin is gray, his eyes faraway and red-rimmed. He's barely fifty years old.

"What's up, Tony? They working you hard?"

"I work all the time now. Have to, to pay the bills."

"I know the feeling."

"What are you doing now? You got a job?"

"Gas'n'Go."

"Yeah?" He looks intrigued by the idea of a career change. "The pay good?"

"You gotta be kidding. Five seventy-five to start. They're hiring, though."

He thinks about it for a second, shakes his head. "I can probably do better here. Not much better," he adds quickly, because he thinks he has insulted me, "but better."

I laugh. Oh, yeah, and did I mention I kill people for money now? Big Tony would probably want that job. Get him off his poor, tired feet for a while, get a decent sum of cash for once. My silence about the killing job is not so much from a sense of self-preservation as from a desire to guard it against the hordes who might take it from me. "Things are tough all over," I say.

"Amen to that." He takes my five. I tell him to keep the change. He looks surprised, and I realize I might have made a mistake, signaled my newfound wealth to anyone in the room. But he just nods gratefully. I was always a good tipper.

I'm on my seventh or eighth when Jeff Zorda comes in and sits next to me. The news is on, more stuff about hospital closings.

Jeff sits down next to me. "What's going on, man? How's the Gas 'em Up?"

"Gas'n'Go. It's fine. How's cable stealing coming along?"

"Slowly but surely. If you weren't such a straight arrow, I'd ask you to partner up with me."

I smile. "Straight arrow? Is that what I am?"

"Yeah. Straight-Arrow Jake. All the loading dock managers used to fix their sheets, take a bribe for extra stuff now and then. You never did."

This is news to me. None of the distributors ever asked me for extra stuff or even offered a bribe. Maybe I had a reputation, and they just stayed away from me. I am strangely flattered by this notion of a Moral Jake which others have formed.

Jeff is staring at the TV. They are doing a piece on the unsolved murder of Corinne Gardocki, showing an old photo of her, smiling innocently. She was a beautiful woman. The killing, according to the reporter, has terrorized the neighborhood. A shocked old woman talks about how terrorized she feels now that one of her neighbors has been killed.

"Ken Gardocki paid someone to kill her," Jeff says, almost conversationally.

I snort, concealing my shock. "Ken? Come on."

"No, he did, I'm sure."

"That was just a Peeping Tom," I argue, wondering where he got his information.

"About two weeks before someone shot her, Ken asked me to do it." Jeff sips his beer and grins. "Guess the next guy took him up on it."

I feel the blood drain from my face. I thought I was Ken's first choice. He told me it had to be me, he just knew it. How many other people had he been through before he got to me?

"Why'd you say no?" I try to act jovial. "What'd he offer you?"

"Offered me ten grand," Zorda said. "Why'd I say no? What, are you kidding? I'm not going to kill people for money. I mean, maybe a little small-time shit here and there, but I went to church when I was a kid. I was raised right."

This is how right Zorda was raised. He took a volunteer job with the ambulance company after the layoffs, he tells me later in the evening, so he would get access to the homes of the sick and dying. When old people who lived alone were taken to the hospital and admitted, he would go back to their apartments or houses the next day and ransack them. He would take credit cards, pills, anything of value. Apparently, in church, when they were telling him it was wrong to kill, they okayed this.

I am back home, drunk and furious. I want to call Ken Gardocki and scream at him, but I know I can't contact him. Why in God's name would he try to hire Zorda before me? I'm smarter than that fuck, and I'm more trustworthy. Straight-Arrow Jake, isn't that what they used to call me? Maybe that was it, because Ken thought I was too much of a straight arrow to even consider the offer. Yeah, that had to be it. Still, next time I see him, he's going to hear about it.

And why did Zorda get offered twice as much money? Does Ken think Jeff's a sharper businessman than me? What the hell's going on? I am too pissed off to think straight. It's almost midnight. I grab the gun from the closet, pull on my gloves, grab some rags and two shopping bags and a small pillow, and head out into the cold.

The Kellner Suites is a three-mile walk. It's snowing again, but just a light dusting, not enough to keep cars off the road but enough to make everything seem quiet on the side streets. Cars pass me and I wonder who is in them, whether or not they have noticed me. Someone called in about me throwing rags into the creek last time, so people are watching. They watch everything, all the time. There are always eyes. The trick is to make them not notice you. I walk without any stride, try to make nothing memorable about myself, just a guy shuffling along the road on his way to nowhere important.

When I see the sign for Kellner Suites off to the side of the highway, I stoop down amid some trees to wrap the rags around my feet. Then I pull the plastic shopping bags over the rags and tie them to my ankles. I don't want the mud on my boots. There are different types of mud, and some scientist in some lab would be able to match the mud from the Kellner Suites parking lot to my boots, and that would be it for this career. The shopping bags make a noise, though, crinkling and rustling every time I take a step. Have to do something about that for next time. Maybe get some canvas bags, and then throw them away. I'm sure not buying new boots every time. These took months to break in.

I go back into the trees at the edge of the parking lot and look for Brecht's car. I've noticed, since my hit-man career began, that almost every building has a little nook or cranny where you can effectively hide. There are so many deserted buildings and crumbling facades around here now that this town is particularly blessed with such hiding places. Once again, I find the darkened treeline to be the best concealment. I don't see Brecht's car anywhere. Working late again, perhaps training his new hire. I crouch as a car pulls into the well-lit parking lot and drives up to the room.

Not Brecht. There is some giggling as a young couple get out and go into one of the other bottom floor rooms.

This is going to be a problem, I realize. Chances are, Brecht will park right up against the well-lit building. With so many spaces available next to the door, why would he park back against the darkened treeline? No, he's going to park in the light, which means I'm going to have to wait in the light. Or run all the way across the lit parking lot with crinkly bags on my feet, shoot him, and then run back the same way, which would be begging for witnesses.

Brecht pulls into the parking lot, and parks right up against the building.

I step forward into the light of the parking lot and freeze there. Dammit. There's nothing I can do. If I started running toward him now, and shot him in his car, it would be too risky. What if he heard me running? Then . . .

Brecht opens the car door quickly and darts up to his room, leaving the engine running and the car door open. He uses his entry card on the lock and darts inside his hotel room. For a panicked second I think he has seen me, has figured out exactly what I'm doing there, and is running inside. But he leaves the hotel-room door open, too. I realize what is happening right away.

Brecht needed to take a piss.

Or a shit maybe. Who knows. That convenience store food'll do it to you. At any rate, I'm running, streaking across the parking lot, maybe forty yards. I do the distance in under ten seconds, taking care not to slip on the ice and snow, my shopping bagged feet crinkling madly. I get up to Brecht's door, and push it open. I can hear the unmistakable sound of a urine stream. He grunts a little. Then I hear a toilet flush.

I close the motel room door and wait for him to come out of the bathroom.

Brecht walks out of the bathroom still zipping up his fly. He is looking down, but notices me in the room pointing a gun at him and he freezes.

"What are you *doing?*"

Bang!

Bits of pillow fly everywhere. DAMMIT! The pillow didn't help worth a damn. My ears are ringing again. Don't use that pillow trick they always show on cop shows. All you do is destroy a perfectly good pillow. I notice also how much smoke is released by a single gunshot. It's like a bomb went off in here. Last time I shot someone I was outside. I got the smell, but the smoke just wafted away and I never noticed it.

Brecht is lying on the ground, his head by the little refrigerator. His glasses have been knocked askew by the fall. His eyes are closed. If he's not dead, he's doing a good impression of someone who is.

There is a good amount of blood on the wall behind us, but nothing has touched me. Pillow flakes are settling all around the silent room. I look at him for a few seconds, thinking deep, philosophical thoughts about him now versus him ten seconds ago, the only difference being those few ounces of lead that have passed through his head, changing everything. Then my hearing starts to return, and I hear the car's engine running outside.

I open the motel room door. But for his running engine, it is complete silence out in the parking lot, no one around. I close the door softly behind me, shut his car off, leaving the keys in the ignition. I see his briefcase on the passenger seat, take it, shut the door and walk off.

Okay, that was stupid. Every time I kill someone, I do something stupid. Last time I kept the gun, this time I steal a briefcase. Why'd I do that? I am walking back out onto the highway with a gun that has killed two people and a dog, and I have a briefcase. If a cop pulled over and started asking me questions about what I'm doing walking around at two in the morning with a briefcase, I'd be completely screwed. I've got to get rid of this shit, but where? I need a place to hide and settle down.

I cross the highway and on the other side is the back of an abandoned discount strip mall. There are dumpsters everywhere. Too perfect. The first place cops would look for stuff to be dumped. I take the bags off my feet, and the rags, and throw those into a dumpster. Just rags and bags, nothing too incriminating. I notice my boots are clean, no mud at all. Very nice. Then, leaning by the dumpster, I decide to open the briefcase.

Inside are a lot of files, pens, calculators and . . . a girlie mag he took from the store. It is called *Juggs and Leggs*. I flip through it. By porn standards, this one is on the low end, the girls worn out ex-strippers and the paper quality barely above newspaper. Why would Brecht, who obviously had access to *Playboy* or *Penthouse*, go so low? Was this his thing, worn out ex-strippers pulling their pussy lips apart for a black-and-white gynecological exam? Guess so. To each his own. Into the dumpster with it. Everything else goes back in the briefcase.

I walk down to the end of the mall and peer around. Nothing but snow falling on a weed-covered parking lot. I go out onto the street, cross it, and walk up into a run-down residential neighborhood where everyone owns a dog, it seems. Every time I pass a house a new animal starts barking. Down a hill, then a gas station, which is closed. But it also has a dumpster, which is almost full. I push the gun down amid some trash bags, walk another few blocks, then dump the briefcase, but first I take out the files. I can't help myself. What could be more damning than walking around with a recently murdered man's files? I tuck the files up under my denim jacket and walk the rest of the way home.

I get home and crack a beer and settle down to read some files. One thing about the late-night convenience store shift, it's killed my sleeping patterns. Now I want to stay up all night and go to bed in the morning.

File one . . . Just a bunch of invoices from distributors. I lay it carefully on a stack of newspapers which I have to take to the dump for recycling. File two is more of the same, and seems to contain a lot of personal stuff, bills, and so on. File three is what I'm looking for, a record of what he's been doing at the store. I flip through it. The first page is a list of what he's accomplished since he has arrived here. Enforced our agreement with Wenke to make all their products more visible, blah blah blah. Then a few printouts of all our timesheets. Then . . . *taadaa* . . . personnel files.

This is what he says about Tommy:

> Tommy Waretka, store manager, was a former factory employee who would be more suited to that kind of work. He lacks the ambition and direction to become a general manager or to move up in the company. He ignores his directives and permits the employees to run the store. I have moved him from management and told him the move is only temporary, but would prefer a more ambitious manager be brought in to allow the store to perform more efficiently.

And another file.

> Kenneth Prezda (Jughead's real name) is a fairly responsible young man who lacks the social skills to operate Gas'n'Go. I would prefer to see him in a largely janitorial role, for which I feel he is better suited. Perhaps we could move him across town to the Wolsely store, and give him a job which requires no customer contact. T. Waretka was overpaying him by over a dollar an hour. I have rectified this.

Last but not least . . .

SINCE THE LAYOFFS 69

Jake Skowran is a former factory manager who feels he is above convenience store work. He is intelligent and, I believe, dangerous. I sense he might be friends with T. Waretka, which is the only reason he was hired, as far as I can tell. His customer service skills are limited and he dislikes authority. I believe he is a heavy drug user (he refused to be drug tested and created a scene at the clinic) and probably the drug boss of the neighborhood. I believe he is still selling drugs out of the store. I have told him to take a week off, and when he returns, I hope to have his job filled.

Well, Brecht just loved us, didn't he? Right about the dangerous thing, though. Too bad no one will ever see these files. Or see Jughead's pay reduction recommendation, which I also find. Or see Tommy's demotion paper, which I also find. Or read Brecht's paranoid fantasy about me being a drug boss. I shove all the files into the stack of newspapers, and put them by the door to run them down to the recycling center at 7 a.m. Then I head into the bathroom to take a piss, and see myself in the mirror.

I have about a thousand little flakes of pillow stuffing stuck in my hair.

Christ. I am covered in evidence. There are pillow-stuffing flakes everywhere. On the couch, by the doorway, on my rain-drenched jacket. I look in the closet for the vacuum cleaner. Gone. Kelly took it with her, said I'd never use it anyway. I have another pillow, just like it. They were a set. I get a knife from the kitchen and cut the fabric on my second pillow, pull out a bit of stuffing. There, that explains that.

No, it doesn't, I realize. They were A SET. One of my pillows is lying by the body of a murder victim, and the matching one is on my couch. Jesus, what was I thinking? I take the second pillow, throw it in a plastic bag, and set about picking up every microscopic flake of pillow stuffing I can find. Then I take a shower, and clean the small bits of stuffing out of the drain. Then I check the couch again, and again, and again. Each time I find a small fiber of pillow stuffing. This is how people get convicted. I need a damned vacuum cleaner.

At seven, I head down to the dump and throw all the files into the recycling bin. Then I buy a new Red Devil vacuum broom at K-mart, go over every last inch of the couch and the living room. Then I go to bed, and sleep the sleep of a man who has finished a job well done.

At about five in the afternoon, Karl, Gardocki's henchman, comes to see me. "Get up," he calls through the door. "Ken wants to see you."

I open the door, cobwebs of a deep sleep still on my brain. "You gotta give me some warning when you're coming over," I tell him angrily. "You can't keep waking me up like this."

"You know how it works," he says, henchmanlike, and goes back down to the SUV to wait for me.

As we're driving out to the bar where I meet Gardocki, Karl asks, "So, you're whackin' people for Mr. G, eh?"

I say nothing. I just stare out the window. Is he offended because he wasn't offered the job? Where did this guy come from? He's not a factory worker, I know that. There's something about him that just doesn't fit in. Who winds up here if they're not from here? This isn't a place people come, it's a place people leave, especially now the factory is gone.

"Where're you from?" I ask.

He says nothing, just stares out the window.

Conversation isn't happening. We drive the rest of the way in silence.

* * *

"Jeff Zorda tells me you asked him first," I say, trying not to sound wounded, but rational. "That puts me in danger. You told me I was the only person you asked."

Gardocki smiles and nods. Nothing rattles him. "I asked Jeff," he says. Gardocki knows why I'm mad, and it has nothing to do with fear of discovery. It is comforting to be understood, even by someone who pays you to kill people. Especially by them.

We are back at the bar off a highway in the middle of nowhere, the bar with no name and a jukebox always playing country songs. The same five guys are playing pool. Ken and I are sitting in a booth away from everyone, and Karl has been sent off to join them. He looks over at us every now and then.

"Why?" I ask. I am almost whining. Gardocki smiles again.

"I mentioned it to him, and he was so enthusiastic about it, I knew I'd made a mistake. So I acted like I was only joking. Then he started acting like he was only joking, too. That's when I decided I had to get someone different, someone like you."

"Like me? What am I like?"

"Honest. Jeff's a scumbag. You can't cheat an honest man, but you can get him to kill people, if he's angry enough. I wanted someone angry, broke, and honest."

I am flattered again. Gardocki knows how to flatter me. "Anyway," he says. "Let's talk about New York."

"Can you get me a silencer? I don't like the gunshot noise. It's dangerous, and it hurts my ears."

He winces. "The factory was loud. What'd you do there?"

"I wore earplugs."

"Wear earplugs, then."

"There's still the noise, though. People can hear it. I'd really like a silencer." Besides, it'd be cool to have a silencer. Isn't that what all hired killers had? What kind of gun-for-hire just walks around with a loud, crappy pistol?

"I'll ask the guys out there. They're going to give you a gun. But if they don't have one, can you get one yourself?"

"I don't know where to get a silencer. Do they sell them at K-mart?"

Ken shrugs. "Have you asked? They sell shotguns there." We look at each other, and burst out laughing.

Being a hired killer, like anything else, has its lighter moments.

I go home, start making dinner, and the phone rings. It is Tommy, from the store.

"Jake, have you seen the news?"

"What news?"

"Turn on Channel Four."

"I don't have a TV." I already know what this is about.

"Jake, man, Brecht got killed. In his hotel room."

Okay, sound surprised. "Brecht? No . . ." No, don't sound grief stricken, that would be too much. "No shit?"

"Someone killed him. Last night."

"Jesus . . ." Go with shocked. And ask the questions someone who hadn't committed the murder would ask. "Was it a robbery?"

"I don't know. They just say it's the second in two weeks. Peeping Tom Murders, they're calling them. Remember Gardocki's wife?"

"Someone was peeping in on Brecht?"

"I guess." Tommy is watching the news, not paying much attention to me. Tommy doesn't care at all about Brecht, probably breathed out a sigh of relief when he heard Brecht was dead. He wouldn't say it, but he does say, "Jesus, I hope I'm not a suspect. I'll tell you, Jake, I didn't care too much for the guy."

"Me either."

"Well, that's fucked up," Tommy says. "Just thought you'd like to know."

"Thanks for calling."

"Sure thing. You coming in Monday?"

"Seven p.m. sharp."

"Come in at six thirty. Brecht started this new thing, we have to come in a half hour earlier now."

"What time do *you* want me in?"

It suddenly occurs to Tommy that since Brecht is dead, none of his company directives have to be heeded. "I want you in at seven," Tommy says cheerfully.

"Seven it is." Tommy is the manager again.

I sit down to dinner and think about this guy I'm going to kill in New York. What did he do, to deserve having me come out there and kill him? Was he a Mafia squealer? I doubt it, because I'm sure they have their own guys to take care of such things. A wife beater, a thief, a drug dealer? Or someone like Brecht, a walking automaton from whom all humanity had been removed for the sake of personal success? I know asking questions about him would be wrong. Part of the job is discretion. One thing I do know is that if he had led a good life, nobody would be willing to shell out ten grand to have me kill him.

So I make up stuff about him. I decide he's a wife-beating, thieving drug dealer who owned a corporation and laid everyone off so he could save himself a few dollars. He's going to get it, all right. Right in the head, one shot.

As I'm taking my last bite, there is a knock on the door. Henchman Karl again. "Jesus, just once, couldn't you call first?"

"No phones. Those are the rules."

I grab my coat. "Let's go."

The ride is the usual thing. "You whackin' people for Gardocki?" Henchman Karl asks.

"Where're you from?"

We drive out there in silence.

Gardocki is furious. He says nothing and doesn't smile. He tells Karl to go play pool (the guy must be a shark by now) and motions to me to come for a walk. Karl watches us go, looking wounded.

We leave the bar and walk out into the dark parking lot, over by some trees. He stares at me for a few seconds before he talks. "What are you, some kind of fucking maniac?"

"What are you talking about?"

"It was the same gun, you dickhead. You used the same gun to kill some guy last night. I just saw it on the news."

"Oh, that."

"Yes that. What's the fucking matter with you? You were supposed to throw it in the creek."

"Ken, they dragged the creek. It was the first place they looked."

"How do you know?"

"I went out there the next day."

"Jesus, you didn't."

"And there were five cops sifting around in the creek. If I'd thrown it in the creek, they'd have the gun now."

"And you knew that."

"It was just lucky."

"You're lucky they didn't see you there."

He stares at me for a few seconds, then throws up his hands in exasperation. "Are you going to kill anyone else with that gun? I'd just like to know."

"I've gotten rid of it."

"Really? Or in two weeks am I going to be watching TV and see that some customer in the convenience store who was rude to you got his brains blown out with my gun—"

"Technically, it was *my* gun. You gave it to me. And no, I'm not a maniac. I've really gotten rid of it this time."

Gardocki shakes his head. "Peeping Tom Murders, that's what they're calling them."

"I know."

Gardocki lights a cigarette. "Who was that guy? What'd he do to you?"

"He was going to fire me."

"From a convenience store? You killed someone because he

was going to fire you from a convenience store? Christ, Jake, I would have found you some work."

"You already did."

"Is this what you want to do, then? Kill people? Because if that's it, I can probably keep you busy."

"Okay, then. Keep me busy."

He looks up at me, stares into my eyes for a few seconds, with the intensity of a lover. He's good with looks. Years of breaking the law have taught him how to unnerve. "I just need to know you got rid of that gun."

"It's gone, I swear."

Gardocki nods. Then he laughs, and slaps me on the shoulder. "You're a crazy bastard," he says. He reaches into his jacket pocket and hands me a piece of paper. "This is the number you call when you get to New York. I said you'd call at three p.m. on Saturday."

"Okay."

"Well, that's it then."

"That's it. Talk to you next week."

"I'll have Karl drive you home."

"I'll take a cab."

Gardocki shrugs. "You got a problem with Karl?"

"He's not my favorite person. Where'd you meet him?"

"Here."

"Where's he from?"

"How the fuck should I know? He said he was out of work a couple of months ago, so I had him deliver packages for me, that kind of thing. Figure he used to work at the factory."

"He didn't. Or if he did, I never saw him there."

Gardocki shrugs again. "You want to shoot some pool while you're waiting for a cab?"

"I'll just wait out here. I like the fresh air."

He turns to go back inside, shaking his head, smiling. "Crazy bastard," he laughs as he staggers across the parking lot. "You're a crazy bastard, Jake."

* * *

I'm a crazy bastard? Look around you, Ken, at a world without rules. There are people whose job it is to drug test convenience store clerks. There are people whose job it is to make sure other people don't bring guns to work. There are people in office buildings right now trying to figure out if laying off seven hundred people will save them money. Somebody right now is promising wealth to someone if they buy a video tape explaining how they can improve their lives. The economy is pain, lies, fear and silliness, and I'm carving myself out a niche. I'm no crazier than the next guy, just more decisive. I think Gardocki knows it. But "You're a decisive bastard" just doesn't sound right.

SIX

The plane touches down at La Guardia and I am giddy with excitement, like a schoolboy on a day trip to the big city. It is 1:15 Saturday afternoon and I have to call these people at three, but what I really want to do is go sightseeing. This is New York City, where every block recalls a scene from some movie I have seen, usually with Kelly. I take a cab downtown and find myself becoming nostalgic in a place I have never been before. I walk down the street where Al Pacino and Ellen Barkin walked in *Sea of Love*. I recognize the storefronts. Then I'm in the neighborhood where Jack Nicholson didn't want to step on cracks in *As Good As It Gets*. I'm having a grand old time until I realize it's time to go kill someone, and maybe also find a place to sleep tonight if I want to go sightseeing tomorrow.

I call the number Ken gave me. A woman answers.

"Hi," I say awkwardly. I wasn't expecting a woman, I was thinking maybe a raspy-voiced mobster with a hard New York accent. This lady sounds like Grace Kelly, and it puts me off guard. "I'm from Wisconsin. Ken Gardocki gave me your number."

"Yes," she says, as if I've just asked for directions to deliver her groceries. "How nice of you to call."

Nice? Is she going to invite me to her garden party? "I suppose you'll need directions," she says cheerfully.

"I'll need directions," I say, at first trying to sound menacing, and then mimicking her polite enthusiasm. "Where are you?"

"Well, you're not coming here," she says, her voice suddenly cold, yet still with the prim accent. "You're going there."

"There. Gotcha."

"It's in Long Island City. Do you know how to get there?"

"No."

"A cab driver will know." She gives me the address, which I copy down. Some street, some number, apartment three. "There will be a man there."

"And he's the one?" The one that gets it, the one to take a bullet?

"Goodness, no," she says, alarmed. "That's Roger's address. He'll explain everything, and give you the other address. And all the . . . equipment."

I realize suddenly that I don't even have a gun. This Roger character must be the guy who gives me the "equipment," which, hopefully, has a silencer attached.

"He's expecting me?"

"Oh, yes. He's expecting you. What time should I tell him you'll be there?"

"How far is it?"

"About a fifteen-minute cab ride from downtown."

"Fifteen minutes then."

"Wonderful," she says, as if we've just planned luncheon. "I hope you had a pleasant flight in."

"Absolutely."

"Very good then."

I find myself talking like her. "Yes. Very good."

How does the likes of Ken Gardocki know this Grace Kelly-like woman? I wonder what she looks like, what this is all about, who Roger is, who is the "one," and what did he do to deserve a visit from me? I'm being paid not to wonder, so I try to stop, but I can't help it. What if he's a guy at one of Grace Kelly's factories who has been causing trouble because the workers there are being mistreated? What would that make me, if I show up and shoot him? An asshole. Like all the others.

I flag down a cab and tell the driver the address, and we drive off. We go over a bridge into a seedy-looking area full of warehouses, trucks and dumpsters, and I immediately start to feel more comfortable. This is the type of place where people who arrange murders live. He starts driving slowly, then pulls up in front of a nondescript brick building under a heavily trafficked bridge.

Inside, the lobby has a musty smell, and crumpled newspapers and packaging are all over the floor. Outside, I can hear a truck beeping as it backs up, people yelling at the driver. There are mailboxes and an intercom, and I'm supposed to be buzzed through a door, but I don't know Roger's last name. I know apartment three, but all the apartment numbers have been ripped off. So I push the third one.

"Yes?" It sounds like an elderly woman.

"Uh . . . Is Roger there?"

She hangs up. I push another button.

"Hello?" Sounds like another woman.

"Hello? I'm looking for Roger." This person hangs up too. What they say about New Yorkers seems to be the case. At any rate, I'm getting sick of this shit and am considering just smashing something through the glass. What kind of asshole hires a killer and doesn't even leave a note for him, or check to make sure the numbers are on the intercom buttons? Then I hear the buzzer go, and I grab the door.

The stairwell is ancient, unpainted. I climb the stairs, which have a faint reek of urine and beer, much like Tulley's. I hear a door open and someone calls down, "You're very punctual."

At the top of the stairs, waiting for me in the doorway, is a thin, very effeminate man slouched, with his hand on his hip, looking me up and down as if I were a runway model. So Roger is not a raspy-voiced middle-aged mobster. He's a flaming queen.

But he's definitely a friendly one. He extends his hand and smiles warmly. "I'm Roger," he says. I shake his hand, not bothering to give my name. "You don't look anything like what I was expecting."

"You either. What were you expecting?"

"Oh, you know, trenchcoat, dark shades, two-thousand-dollar Armani suit. That sort of thing. Like in the movies." He backs away from the door. "Please, come in." He ushers me into a warmly lit and exquisitely decorated apartment, plants and paintings everywhere, jazz playing softly on the stereo. I was thinking the inside of the apartment would be as run down as the stairwell, but Roger has been taking care of the place.

"I must say," he starts out, "I just think it's so neat to meet someone like you."

"Someone like me?" What does that mean? A straight guy? Someone from Wisconsin? A loading dock manager?

"You know . . ." Roger looks awkward, and I suddenly see what he is trying to say.

"Oh, a killer."

He looks relieved. "Yes, a killer. It's so . . . neat." He pauses. "I really was expecting a black Armani suit, though." My slovenly blue jeans have disappointed him.

"And sunglasses," I finish for him.

"Yes, and sunglasses."

"Why?"

"Because that's always what they wear in the movies."

"Don't you think it would be smart not to dress like everyone's idea of a killer?"

This profound piece of brilliance impresses Roger no end. He stares at me, awestruck. Roger thinks talking to a hired killer in his living room is a hoot. I need to put a stop to this, pick up my pistol, get the address and be on my way. I adopt my serious, hired-killer expression. "I'm here to get a gun and an address," I say.

"Oh, right, right." Roger laughs. He waves his hands around, almost flirtatiously, giggling. "I'll be right back." He darts off into his bedroom and returns holding a pistol, which he is carelessly pointing right at me. I sidestep slightly, to get away from the barrel, an instinct born of hating guns, and Roger puts his hand to his mouth in shock over his own carelessness.

"I'm so sorry," he says.

"It's all right," I say. He hands me the gun and I motion toward the table. "Just put it down. I have to put gloves on first."

He nods. "Yes, of course."

"You might want to wipe your prints off it, too."

Once again, he is awestruck by my brilliance. I see now why he has hired me. He doesn't seem to have much of a sense of intelligent criminal behavior.

"What should I use," he asks, "to get rid of the prints?"

"A rag."

He bursts out laughing. "A rag!" I have scored points for being a criminal genius. He gets a rag from the kitchen, and begins to polish the gun from barrel to handle, then gently, ceremoniously, lays it on the kitchen table. I stare at it. It is cheap and tinny looking and there is no silencer.

"How many bullets are in it?"

"I'm not sure," he says. "You'll only need one, right?"

"I don't know," I say, as I pull a pair of gloves on and pick up the pistol.

My answer seems to have disturbed him.

"I only want you to shoot him once," Roger says nervously, the giggling flirtiness replaced by worry and fear. "I don't want him hurt. Just killed."

I find the little latch that releases the magazine, and it slides into my palm with an expertness that I don't possess. Roger's conviction that I am an experienced gun handler appears strengthened by this accidental show of dexterity, and I examine the magazine as Roger stares at me. He is waiting for reassurance. The magazine is full.

"I've never needed a second bullet for a hit," I say truthfully, professionally. "But once I got attacked by a dog."

"Jason doesn't have a dog," Roger says.

"That's a relief." I pull back the slide and cock the pistol, and am about to put the gun in my pocket when I realize what I have just done. The slightest jolt would send a bullet right into my own spleen. I gently click the hammer forward, un-cocking it, then slip it into my coat, acting like it was a test I always perform before carrying out my work. Roger is still waiting for me to reassure him I am not going to make a mess of the victim.

"I only want him shot once," Roger says again.

"Hopefully, that will do the trick," I say. "You never really know until the time. He might put up a fight."

"He won't put up a fight," says Roger.

"Well, I doubt he's just going to stand there and let me shoot him," I say.

"He'll lie there," says Roger. "He'll be sedated."

"He'll be sedated?"

"He has AIDS," says Roger. "He's dying. He knows you're coming. But you have to go between five and seven. That's when the nurse leaves for dinner. She drugs him up. I thought you knew this."

"How the hell would I know this?"

Now Roger looks upset. Roger begins to realize that I really am a killer, that I would even kill someone who wasn't already dying

if the money was right. Up until now, it seems, he has been thinking of me as a public service professional, or a mercy killer like Dr.
Kevorkian. Who, incidentally, he should have hired.

"So Grace didn't tell you anything?"

"She told me where you lived, that was it."

"Oh my," says Roger. "You know you have to steal something?"

"What?"

"You have to steal something from his apartment. To make it look
like a burglary. That way the insurance will pay for all his treatment."

"I don't like to steal things," I tell him. "I'm not a thief."

"You won't actually be stealing it. Just take something valuable.
You have to smash the lock and take something," Roger says, and
he sounds like he is beginning to panic. "I thought Grace
explained all this . . . Oh no, oh no . . ."

I groan. "Settle down," I say, trying to sound soothing. "We'll just
go over all the details to make sure we've got everything right."
Roger appears calmed by my paternal manner, so I keep it up, playing the kind-hearted, understanding hired killer. I certainly don't
want him freaking out, but I also realize that I'm being paid here,
that I work for him. It really isn't that different from having someone call the loading dock, freaking out because they're worried
about their shipment of machine-tooled tractor parts being lost. Service is service.

I sit down at the kitchen table. "Now," I say, firmly. "Start from
the beginning."

Here's the deal: Jason is a friend of Roger's and he is dying of AIDS.
That much I've figured out already. Jason and Roger have figured
that if Jason dies during the commission of a burglary, rather than
passing away in his sleep, some kind of homeowner's policy will
pay his estate enough money to cover the cost of the last year of
his treatment. Jason has about a week to live anyway. Grace is in
on this because she was Jason's co-signer on some kind of hospital

admission form, and the hospital is going to come after her for the bill. Despite her accent, I'm told, Grace doesn't have a whole lot of money, and the ten grand the three of them have scraped together for me is about all they can come up with. Ten grand. So Gardocki is keeping a $2,500 finder's fee. Fine with me.

As I am leaving, Roger suddenly realizes the finality of everything and bursts into tears. I tell him to take a walk, get to a bar or something where he'll have an alibi, as he'll likely be a suspect for a day or two. Once again, he gives me that awestruck look, a respect for my criminal mind. He runs down the street behind me as I walk off. He is sobbing like a child. I wonder how he'll stand up to an interrogation, if it comes to that, and am glad he knows nothing about me.

I find the apartment, which is only about two blocks from Roger's place and in an almost identical building. I go around back to the fire escape, looking at my little hand-drawn map, and see everything as I was told. The fire escape has been left in the down position for me, the rear window is open. I climb up to the third floor and look through the filthy window. Sure enough, in a dark room with paint peeling off the walls there is a man dying in his bed.

The window slides open, and I climb in. I look around the room and think, this is not how anyone should die, in a room like this, peeling paint, faded carpet with a damp and musty odor. I see the chair where the nurse has been sitting. There is a book there, some knitting, things to keep her busy while she watches this man die. Perhaps she gets up every now and then to fiddle with knobs on one of these machines. I look at a chart lying by the bed while some breathing apparatus pumps oxygen into him, an almost soothing rhythm, hiss, pump, hiss, pump. The chart says he was born the same month and year as I was, and it's all over for him. This could have been my life. I look at his birthplace: Omaha, Nebraska. Gardocki's hometown. A Midwesterner. I feel some kind of kinship with him. Maybe he came here because he was gay.

I know people in my neighborhood aren't too open-minded about shit like that.

Anyway, like me, he got fucked by circumstance and left to die. Circumstance did a more thorough job on him, though. I'm here because an insurance company fucked him. I'm here because a giant corporation fucked me. There is a broke ex-loading dock manager standing in a dying gay actor's room, with a pistol, because of big business decisions made years or months before.

His eyes are closed, and he appears to be sleeping peacefully. No pain, anyway. I aim the pistol at his chest.

"Later, dude," I tell him.

BANG.

A fountain of blood spurts from his chest. He sighs heavily. Then there is another spurt, much smaller this time. Then a third, smaller still, then some blood pooling in the sheets. He sighs again. He's dead. One shot, just like I promised.

There's some smoke in the room, but not as much as I remember from before. Maybe it's the gun, or maybe I'm just getting used to it. The noise with this gun was almost as bad, though, and my ears ring. No more shooting people without a silencer, I promise myself. Absolutely, must, get a silencer. Note to self: Try *Soldier of Fortune* Magazine. I'm sure they sell them there, isn't that what Gardocki suggested?

Okay, time to go break and steal stuff.

I wander around, dump out a few drawers, looking for something valuable to steal. There's an old candlestick holder in a pewter stand. No self-respecting burglar would bring that to a pawn shop. The television looks like the last show it picked up clearly was *Bonanza,* back when it was on prime time. Besides, it's one of those three hundred pound affairs from the '70s when TVs were furniture. I dig around some more. Some old towels, a busted coffee maker. Shit, this guy isn't exactly Howard Hughes. I figure if there was anything valuable, from what I know of human nature, the nurse probably helped herself to it some time back. I smash the lock on the

door and kick some stuff around for a while, then decide I've had
enough of this and slide the window open to leave . . .

BEEEEEEP! BEEEEEEP! BEEEEEEP!

Goddamn, what a racket! My first thought is that the window is
alarmed, but I remember I came in this way. What kind of alarm
only goes off when you're leaving? Then I notice it appears to be
coming from the wall beside the bed. It's one of his life support sys-
tems. Just a tad late. I look around to see how to turn the damned
thing off.

BEEEEEEP! BEEEEEEP! BEEEEEEP!

Jesus, this'll bring cops, it's so damned loud. Is the nurse deaf?
Where's the setting for this thing? I see it on the far wall, and there
are more controls there than a 747's flight panel. By the time I figure it out there'll be a SWAT team in the lobby. I pick up the pewter
candle holder and hurl it at the thing which appears to be making
the noise. It ricochets off the wall and hits poor Jason in the head.

"Fuck!" I scream.

The plug is under the bed, but I can't get under the bed, there
isn't room, and . . .

BEEEEEEP! BEEEEEEP! BEEEEEEP!

. . . there's no way I'm getting *on* the bed because it's soaked in
blood, and AIDS blood at that. I can't leave the apartment with this
noise going off. Shit.

There's a breaker panel on the far wall. I run over, pull it open
and slam shut every breaker.

BEEEEEEP! BEEEEEEP! Beee . . .

Thank God. Silence fills the room. I can hear my own panicked
breathing. I listen for sounds in the hallway. Nothing.

I walk over to the window, where noises from the street are fil-
tering up. Trucks are going by, an air horn goes off. In the distance,
I can hear a train clattering along tracks, from above there is the
roar of a jet approaching La Guardia. Life goes on in the big city.
No one has even noticed this little disturbance.

I hop out the window, climb down the fire escape, and in a few seconds I am back out in the street, my heart still pounding. I walk away, taking care to walk normally, in a way no one will notice. I see a dumpster, look around quickly, and drop the gun in it.

I find myself suddenly exhausted by all this crap, the need to walk normally, to not be noticed, the obsession with evidence. This killing people, it's a job, and I need a day off. Screw sightseeing. I call a cab and head to the airport, wishing I was already at Tulley's.

Ten hours later, I am.

There is actually a crowd here, because Tony Wolek, God bless him, has arranged a darts league, and tonight is the night of the big championship. With shit falling apart everywhere, Tony has appointed himself the morale officer of the town. Now he organizes things that he thinks will keep people's spirits up. He encouraged some talentless teenagers to start a band and play on Friday nights. He hosted a costume party with a best-costume contest for Halloween. All these events have done fairly well, considering, and as I get progressively drunker at the bar, I find myself feeling some love for the guy, for the decent way he never stops trying. Then I see him, gray-faced, as he hands a beer to an underage kid and I think again that he doesn't have long to live, another battle casualty of the layoffs.

I get a whiff of perfume, and look around to see a woman with thick black hair leaning up against the bar, waiting to get Tony's attention. I remember her from the factory secretarial pool, remember on several mornings admiring her legs and ass while walking behind her up the factory drive, at 6:55 a.m., back when we had jobs. The beer compels me to tell her this fascinating bit of information.

"I remember you," I say, and stop before I get to the ass and legs part.

She looks around at me, studies me for a second without expression. I thought she was pretty then, but now after months of womanlessness, I think she is positively beautiful. I wonder if it's possible for a fairly drunk guy watching ESPN highlights to make a positive impression. I doubt it. She keeps looking at me but doesn't smile.

"Yeah," she says. "From the factory."

Her voice is smoky and a little rough, which turns me on. Then, if it was completely different, say high-pitched and squeaky, that would turn me on, too. Pretty much everything about her turns me on. It also turns me on that she takes a long swig of her beer and keeps looking at me, as if she is now expecting the great pick-up line that will sweep her off her feet.

"Nice seeing you again," I say. Brilliant. Okay, I'm out of practice.

"You too." She doesn't leave. I'm sure there is at least one man over at the darts game waiting for her to return, but she doesn't seem in any particular hurry. And she's only bought a beer for herself. And she's still looking at me. I'm being given a chance. But my mind's still a blank. This whole thing kind of came out of nowhere. I wasn't ready, I want to start over, I need to do a little mental preparation.

She looks at me. I look back. Finally she pushes away from the bar and quickly says, "Seeya" and is gone. My chance is over. I blew it. I try to catch a glimpse of her fine ass as she disappears into the crowd, hoping she'll turn around and give me a knowing, over-the-shoulder glance, but she is gone.

I want to bang my head on the bar. I have a sinking feeling, sure that everyone else in the room must have noticed my humiliating idiocy. I look around. Everyone is still doing what they were doing. The place is exactly the same. Only I have changed.

"How was New York?" It's Ken Gardocki, calling me from a pay phone at 8 in the morning.

"Busy town. Full of people," I tell him. As usual, he has woken me from a deep sleep.

"How'd everything go?"

I realize that this isn't a social call. "Oh, fine. Everything went fine."

"According to plan?"

"According to plan."

"I've got something else for you."

"Jesus." I hadn't expected to be put to work again so quickly. Or even ever. At least one major marketplace around here is booming. I've gotten in on the ground floor at just the right time, as the business analysts say. "Already?"

"This one's kind of a rush job," Ken says.

"No problem."

"Come round the bar tonight."

"See you there."

"I'll send Karl."

"Good. I've missed him."

I get up, stretch, look out the window at the snowy back yard, the dying tree and the rusted tool shed, and realize that in my sock drawer I now have almost three thousand dollars, and Ken Gardocki owes me five thousand more, which he's probably going to give me tonight. I am no longer poor.

But the mind-set of poverty sticks around longer than the poverty itself. Therefore, I still find myself planning to go down to the convenience store and ask Tommy for cigarettes, even though I could buy a truckload of them. I still have a moment of stress when I think that my little old car is running low on gas and needs new tires. I could buy a much better car just with what I have in the sock drawer, I know, but the stress is still there.

I know, now, how quickly it can disappear, all of it. Not just the money, but the life, the stability. None of it is real. The poor know this. That is why they so rarely invest, or do anything with money which will net them more money. Investing in the future is a luxury of the rich. The poor just look for ways to make the present bearable. Money can provide moments of pleasant reality, be what they may. It's why money never moves into different hands. Ways to blow all the cash in the drawer go through my mind, as I imagine myself across a table from last night's mystery girl at the bar, in a fine restaurant, encouraging her to order the most expensive bottle of wine. Then I imagine a giant bag of coke for me and Tommy and a few other guys, a night out, some high-priced call girls . . .

I start thinking about that. Hmmm. I lie back in bed and wonder how much a night with two high-priced call girls goes for, anyway. Are there any left in this town? Probably not. I'm sure they left with the money. Probably the day the factory closed. I wonder if that's a leading economic indicator that Wall Street minds have already thought of, the migration of high end pros. Maybe there's some anthropologist somewhere who tags them and follows their movements on a giant map so they can find out where the money is, the best place to open restaurants and car dealerships. It sure ain't here.

Whatever. No call girls for me. I'm going to find out if Tommy knows anything about the secretary with the raspy voice.

"How're things, man?" I shake Tommy's hand exuberantly as I step behind the counter down at the convenience store. He looks like the Tommy I remember, now Brecht is gone. He has a spring in his step and a ready smile.

"The cops were round here. They wanted to talk to you," he tells me.

"To me? Why? They think I killed the fucker?" I laugh at the absurdity of the idea, but Tommy doesn't laugh with me.

"Dude, I think they do."

"They think I killed Brecht?" I am going a little pale, but I think even an innocent man would get nervous about the idea of being suspected of murder by the police, so I don't try to act otherwise.

"They said that Brecht sent an e-mail to the company head-quarters asking someone, a private investigator or something, to do a background check on you."

"On me? Why?"

"I don't know. It was his last e-mail. You'd better go down and talk to them."

I act like this news has stunned me. It has. Little Fucker Brecht was looking for a reason to fire me, wanted to turn up some drug history. I have no police record. He would have fired me anyway, though. I know that now that I've read his files, but he was look-ing for something specific. Shit. Hadn't thought of that. Anyway, I suppose I'd better go down to the station.

"Hey, when's my next shift? I still work here, right?"

"Of course, man. Come in tomorrow at seven o'clock."

"See you then," and I add a joke. "If I'm not in jail for murder."

Tommy doesn't laugh.

Fuck.

I'm driving over to the police station, thinking, the very idea of being a suspect for anything has never even really occurred to me. I haven't practiced answers in front of a mirror because I didn't imagine anyone would be able to put pieces together to come up with anything. I imagined the police department would be in the same disarray as everything else, underfunded, indifferent. Hospi-tals were closing, restaurants were closing, even discount retailers were shutting their doors. Why were the police stations staying open? But here they were. The need to punish the local populace for their misdeeds is obviously more important than the need to heal, feed and clothe them.

But now I'm going to have to practice answers. I drive slowly. Where have I been? New York. No point lying about that, it's on flight information. Why did I go there? To sightsee? How many job-less, broke men fly across the country to go sightseeing? Bad answer. To visit my sick aunt? I'll need a sick aunt if they check, some hospital records, something. I have to go to the library, get a New York phone book and look up Skowrans, claim one of them is a cousin or something. How about for a job interview? Then they'll ask which firm. Aaaaargh. Why didn't I think of this sooner?

I get to the police station, and notice how nice the building is. The parking lot has just been paved. Every cent of government funds is going to crime fighting, it seems. The *NYPD Blue* sets which I've become accustomed to seeing on television, with their dirty unpainted walls, are nowhere to be seen. The floors are clean, the desks new, the lighting perfect. The lady cop in the lobby sits behind a smooth, neatly rounded desk which accents the whole feng shui of the place. They've brought in an interior decorator, I think, to make the newly arrested prostitutes and petty criminals feel comfortable during their bookings.

"I've been asked to show up," I tell the woman, as if I couldn't imagine a more preposterous thing. "They want to talk to me."

"About what?"

"Ahh . . . Someone was killed at my place of work. Well, not *at* my place of work, but—"

"So, Homicide," she says. "You want to talk to Homicide."

I don't want to talk to anyone, I'm about to say. They want to talk to me. But I just nod, and she gets on the phone and rings someone. There is a brief conversation, and she turns to me.

"What's your name?"

"Jake Skowran."

"What's the name of the victim?"

"Errr . . ." I act momentarily like it's of no consequence to me, then finally come up with it. "Brecht, I think."

She repeats this information into the phone, then tells me to have a seat. I sit on a plush leather couch, surrounded by well-cared-for plants, and watch people come and go for a few minutes.

Then I see her.

The girl from the bar last night. In a police uniform. She's a freakin' cop! She pulls open the glass door and walks right past me.

"Hi," I say, to get her attention.

She looks down, recognizes me. "Oh, hi."

"I saw you in Tulley's last night."

"Yeah, I remember." Her voice is still smoky rough, and again it turns me on. I like the way she looks straight at me when she talks. "What're you doing here?"

Okay, good question. What am I doing here? "Parking tickets," I say quickly, my first experience with lying to the police.

"That's Building One, downtown," she says helpfully. "You're in the wrong place." She starts giving me directions when a big, muscular man in a perfectly pressed white shirt and a shoulder holster comes up behind us and interrupts.

"Mr. Skowran?"

"Yes?"

She stops talking, quickly realizing that I've fibbed about the parking tickets. My first attempt at lying to the police did not go well.

"I'm Detective Martz. You can come this way." He motions for me to follow him.

"Nice seeing you again," I tell her.

"Yeah," she says.

"Say, what's your name, by the way?"

"Officer Zadow." She points to her name tag.

"No, your first name."

"Sheila."

"Sheila. That's a nice name." I'm about to be interrogated about a murder I've committed and I'm trying to pick up a cop in the lobby of the police station. I look at her left hand for a ring, and don't see anything. I give her my warmest Jake smile. "I hope to see you at Tulley's again sometime."

"I'll be there Thursday," she says. "The darts tournament finals."

"Excellent. See you there," I say, as if she's just agreed to a date. I turn to Detective Martz, who is waiting patiently. "Let's talk," I say.

Here's what the cops do with me.

Detective Martz leads me along a maze of corridors and asks me to sit in a room with two chairs. The walls are yellow cinder blocks, and I sit and stare at them for fifteen minutes, until finally the door opens, and another detective, who doesn't introduce himself, comes in holding a file.

"Are you Mr. Kendrick?" he asks. Before I can say no, he says, "No, Mr. Kendrick is black." He nods to himself, happy to have sorted that out. Then he leaves. Five minutes after that a third detective opens the door and says, "Mr. Skowran?"

"Yeah?"

"Come with me, please."

We go about five feet down a corridor to a different room, where he asks me to wait for a minute. This room is identical, except there are two chairs AND a table. I sit with elbows resting on the table for ten minutes, wondering if this is some kind of cop trick, faking you into thinking they're so disorganized they couldn't catch a killer if he walked in here and screamed "I'm the Killer!," some kind of false-sense-of-security thing, then they spring it on you that they know everything, they're all really smart and well organized. I notice a pen on the table, and I stare at it for a few minutes. "Shawford Industries" is written on the pen, with a phone number. I remember Shawford Industries, a business park a half hour north of here which closed shortly before our plant did. I practice balancing the pen on my nose for a few minutes, then inexplicably start chewing on it. Then I put it down, just as the door opens.

It is yet another detective. "Mr. Skowran?"

"Yes?"

"I'm sorry, the detective investigating the Brecht homicide isn't here at the moment."

"What do you want me to do?"

"Could you call him later today?"

"Do you have his number?"

The detective hands me a business card. "Thank you for coming in," he says.

"Yeah, sure." I had nothing better to do with this hour than sit in different chairs and chew pens, I almost say, but don't.

I say goodbye nicely and throw the business card in the lobby trash can on my way out the door. The trash can appears to be hand-carved wood. That's where the local government funds are going.

I'm back at home feeling safe (my opinion of the local police is even lower than usual) when Karl comes by. This time, for once, I'm wide awake.

"Karl, my man. Good to see you," I lie.

He nods, almost smiles. He's being suspiciously more pleasant than usual. We go down to the car, and he strikes up a conversation.

"Where you been? Haven't seen you in a few days."

"Where're you from?" I am rifling through my pockets, looking for a ball point. "Damn. Have you got a pencil on you? I gotta write a note."

Karl is quiet for a few seconds, then finally says, "I'm from Shawford. I used to work at Shawford Industries, but I got laid off."

I'm about to tell him about my twice-in-one-day experience with the name Shawford Industries when he cuts me off. "Stole plenty of pens on my way out the door, though," he says. He pulls a pen from his jacket pocket and hands it to me.

I'm looking at a Shawford Industries pen for the second time that day. It's the same pen. It has my teeth marks on it.

I'm staring at the pen, just staring, blankly, wondering what to make of this, when Karl says, "Hey buddy, can I have my pen back if you're not gonna use it?"

I give it back to him.

"Did you steal anything from your place when you got the axe?" he asks jovially. I know right away there is something wrong with this. Karl never got laid off.

"Uh-uh," I say. Karl starts chattering on about how wonderful it is to steal stuff from work. I nod as if I'm listening, but I'm trying to think. I'm thinking, Karl has been in the police station today. I'm thinking, Karl has been in the police station today because he works there.

There is no other explanation.

We pull up to Ken Gardocki's little hangout, the bar off in the woods in the middle of nowhere, just as it is starting to snow. Gardocki is in the parking lot, playing with a rottweiler puppy who is bounding around, trying to catch snowflakes. He waves at me as I get out of the car.

"Jake, how ya doin'? Look at this little guy."

I watch the puppy for a few seconds. No doubt he is cute, but there is an undercover cop right behind me, just waiting for one of us to slip up, say something which will let everything out of the bag. Is he wearing a wire? Karl is standing only a foot from my left shoulder, almost breathing down my neck as I watch the puppy. The invasion of space bothers me.

"Ken, I'd like to talk to you for a second," I say finally, when I think he's just going to play with the damned dog all night.

"Sure, Jake. I want to talk to you, too." The puppy comes up to me and starts bouncing around on my boots, waiting for my attention. I stare straight ahead.

I take a step toward Gardocki, and Karl follows. I turn around and say, politely, "Could you go inside for a minute? Me and G got something personal we need to talk about."

Karl takes a step back but doesn't go into the bar. The puppy gives up on me, runs up to Karl, and he starts playing with it.

"He's a cutie, isn't he?" Gardocki says. "I just got him today. I'm calling him Rufus Junior."

"What happened to Rufus Senior?" asks Karl, who knows damned well what happened to Rufus Senior. He gave me the gun to do it, he hangs out with Gardocki all the time, he knows Gardocki's wife and dog have passed away. He's just asking to get something on tape, I figure. Before Ken can give any kind of answer, I wheel around on him.

"Are you fucking deaf? I just asked you to go into the bar?"

"Hey, man . . . " he starts to protest. I guess he figured our bonding session, where he told me all about stealing pens from an imaginary factory he never worked in, had made us friends for life.

"Easy, Jake," says Gardocki, finally taking his attention from the puppy and turning to me. "What the hell's the matter with you?"

I am still staring at Karl. "Get in the fucking bar. Leave us alone."

"I don't take orders from you—"

"Ken, will you tell this asshole to get in the fucking bar so we can talk?"

Gardocki and Karl look at each other for a few seconds, then Gardocki nods at him. "We'll be inside in just a few minutes," he tells Karl. "Why don't you order us a pitcher of beer."

Karl walks off into the bar, giving me what he probably imagines is a hard stare. I watch him go until the door is closed behind him.

"Ken, that guy is a cop."

"Oh, shit, Jake. You've never liked him."

"And now I know why. Because he's a cop. He was down at the police station today."

Gardocki thinks about this for a second. "What were *you* doing down at the police station?"

"The cops asked me to come and talk to them."

"About what?"

"The guy from the convenience store, Brecht. I'm a suspect."

"You stupid asshole, I told you to throw that gun away—"

"You're missing the point. Karl was there. He was at the police station."

Gardocki shrugs. "You were at the police station. Does that mean you're a cop?"

I put my head in my hands and walk in a circle, and the puppy starts bouncing around my feet. I kick it, and it thinks I'm trying to play, so I kick again, harder. The puppy yelps.

"*Hey!*" Gardocki yells. "What's the matter with you? You already shot one of my dogs . . ."

I pause for a second and take a deep breath. "Did you hear what you just said?"

Gardocki is comforting the puppy. It is wagging its tail madly, looking at me with doubt.

"That's exactly the type of slip-up he's waiting for, Ken. He's wearing a wire, I guarantee it."

Gardocki is thinking. The man isn't stupid, he's been a criminal in this town for a quarter of a century. All the drugs and gambling go through him. He didn't get to where he is by not considering every angle, and I can see now that I've cracked something, that he is really considering the idea that Karl might be a cop.

"How did you meet him?" I ask.

"In a bar. Tulley's. About five months ago. He said he needed work. He was with a guy from Shawford that I knew, guy who used to bring down drugs from Canada. The guy vouched for him."

I think for a second. "That guy must have got busted. He made a deal. Introduce you to Karl for a free ride. The drugs, the gambling. They wanted you for something. They knew you were the closest thing this town has to a mob boss. He set you up."

Gardocki is far away, thinking hard. "I haven't seen that guy since," he says. "You might be right."

"I *am* right."

Gardocki goes over to his sports car, opens the trunk, and takes out something wrapped in an oily rag. He hands it to me. I don't even need to unwrap the rag. I know the weight by now. I put the bulky pack in my inside coat pocket.

"Let's go talk to Karl," he says.

We go into the bar, where Karl is waiting to order beers. Gardocki puts a hand on his shoulder and says, "Let's just get a couple of six-packs and head out to my lodge."

Karl shrugs, orders the six-packs, and Gardocki pays for them.

We get in and Gardocki motions to Karl that he is driving. I get in the back seat and Gardocki pulls out onto the small, winding country road and turns away from the town. We drive out into increasing wilderness as the snow starts coming down harder.

"You've got a lodge out here?" Karl asks, and I wonder if I hear anything in his voice other than curiosity.

Gardocki nods and turns up the radio. We drive on for a few more minutes, and I don't see a single car on the road in either direction, just increasing snowfall.

"We going to the Upper Peninsula?" asks Karl, and this time I'm sure I hear fear. Like he is trying to control it. Gardocki pulls the car over onto the shoulder. "Gotta take a leak," he says. "Anyone else?" He looks at me.

"Yeah," I say, and hop out. It is quiet out, except for the nearly inaudible hiss of snow falling into the pines all around us. Gardocki walks over to a ditch, and I find a spot a few feet away. I'm expecting him to say something to me, something that Karl isn't supposed to hear, but Karl hops out of the car and stands between us. Either he thought he was being excluded from a conversation or he really needed to piss, I don't know.

I never find out. I step back, walk behind Karl, take out the gun and shoot him in the back of the head.

BANG.

Karl falls forward into the ditch.

"AAAARGH!" Gardocki screams. He jumps back, still holding his dick in his hand. "What the fuck are you doing?"

"I shot him, Ken. Wasn't that the idea?"

"You crazy fucking maniac! You madman! What's the matter with you?" Gardocki is staring at me, pale. "I wanted to talk to him."

"About what?"

"About whether or not he was a cop. Remember that, Jake?"

"And you thought he was going to be completely honest with you?" I put the gun in my jacket pocket, and look at Gardocki. "Will you put your dick away?"

Gardocki puts his dick away, and goes over to the ditch and looks down at Karl. "Jesus," he mutters. Then he looks back at me. Despite a life of criminal behavior, I doubt he has ever seen a dead body before or witnessed the death itself. For me this is old hat.

I step down into the ditch and grab Karl's jacket, and pull up his shirt, looking for the wire. Nothing. I grab his wallet out of his coat pocket, flip through it. A Wisconsin driver's license. Karl Ravech-eska. A bowling league membership card. Eighty dollars in cash, four twenty-dollar bills. That's it. Not much of a wallet. I toss the wallet up to Ken.

Ken flips through it. "There's nothing here to make me think he was a cop," Ken says.

I roll Karl over, still looking for the wire. "What'd you expect? His membership card to the Police Athletic League? It's called under-cover, Ken. It's what you don't see that's important. No pictures of loved ones, no supermarket discount card, no library card. That license was all the fake ID the cops could be bothered to make. That's a fake wallet. His real one's probably back at the police sta-tion." I go through Karl's pockets. Cigarettes. Coins. Lint.

"There's no wire, is there?" asks Gardocki.

"Not yet." Now it occurs to me for the first time that I might have made a mistake, and Gardocki senses the doubt.

"You just shot my assistant," he says. "You shot my assistant, my wife, my dog, your boss . . ."

"You paid me to shoot your wife," I say, not really paying attention to him. I am starting to sweat now, the notion of having killed someone for no reason starting to swell in my mind. I don't want to show Gardocki my face, so I keep turned away from him. For reasons I'm not sure of, I unlace and pull off Karl's right boot.

"Are you going to shoot everybody in this town?" Gardocki says.

"Time will tell." I shake out the right boot. Nothing. I unlace the second boot and pull it off.

"What the fuck are you doing? Undressing him?"

I shake out the second boot. A small piece of laminated plastic falls out into the snow. I pick it up and look at it.

"Here you go," I say, handing the card to him.

"Karl Grohleiter," Gardocki reads off the card. "Wisconsin State Police. Well, I'll be damned."

I hop out of the ditch. "Let's get outta here. Snow'll cover him in a couple of hours."

We are driving back through what has become a blizzard, not talking, listening to the radio jock describe the blizzard to us. "It's really coming down," he tells me, as I peer out the window. I can't see a thing because it's really coming down. The snowstorm play-by-play is somehow comforting.

"We just killed a cop," says Gardocki.

"Yeah," I say.

"That's death penalty."

"There's no death penalty in Wisconsin."

"Really?" This seems to cheer him up. I've never understood that, why some people are so afraid of the death penalty. I'm afraid of life in prison. After I took my first job, Gardocki's wife, I went to the library and looked up the death penalty, and was disappointed to find that Wisconsin didn't have it.

"Anyway," I say. "The only way it can be traced to us is by the people at the bar who saw him with us."

"They'll be fine," Gardocki says. "I've known those guys for years. They're good youpers." UPers, Upper Peninsula country folk who like to drink and mind their own business. I'm not convinced.

"Let's get a story together just in case."

"Okay." Gardocki is looking to me for advice now. He respects my opinion and experience in these matters, now that my judgment about Karl has proven correct. It is a good feeling, to have someone respect your input, a feeling I haven't experienced since the factories closed. I have become an indispensable partner to the richest criminal in town.

"What was this rush job you wanted to see me about?"

Gardocki is lost in thought. He snaps out of it. "Oh, that, yeah." He pulls a piece of paper out of his back pocket and hands it to me. "Miami. You have to be there next weekend."

"Miami?"

"Yeah." Gardocki is tired, distracted. The cop-shooting thing has really got to him. "Let's talk about it tomorrow."

"Sure."

The next morning, before I contact Gardocki, I go over to the convenience store to get my schedule. Tommy is behind the counter, reading some important-looking memo with the Gas'n'Go logo emblazoned across the top.

"They're trying to sell this store," he says. "Do you believe this shit? We're going to get laid off *again*."

I look at the memo. It is an invitation to prospective buyers to franchise the store. Gas'n'Go 818 is going on the auction block. The rest of the memo is corporate blather about how the loss of Brecht is a blow to all humanity, especially starving children, and how the necessary redistricting is causing the company to sell off some stores in his area. If the store isn't sold by February first, it will be demolished.

There is a list of all the stores to be sold, and the list has two names on it: ours, and the Wolsely store, which is also in a bad neighborhood. Gas'n'Go doesn't want any more potential executives getting bullets through their heads in our town. They're unloading their ghetto interests.

"How much they want for the place?"

"A franchise is forty thousand."

"Let's buy the place. You and me."

Tommy shrugs. "Twenty thousand each?"

"Yeah."

"You're going to have to lend me twenty thousand, because I can't even pay my mortgage right now. Oh, wait, you make less than I do here and your TV just went to the pawnshop. So I'll have to say no to that one."

"I can get the money."

Tommy looks at me. "How're *you* gonna get the money, Jake?"

"I can get the money."

"Jake, this is bullshit. Look at you, you're stealing cigarettes, you must owe bookies what, five grand, you—"

"I'll get the money."

Tommy stops talking, looks at me. He takes a pack of cigarettes from the rack, stealthily, so the cameras won't see him (though it's doubtful they'll send another executive down here to view the tapes) and motions for me to go outside.

We step outside, where the sun is blinding, reflecting off the night's new-fallen snow. Cars and trucks hiss by.

"Where are you gonna get the money, Jake?"

"I can get it. By February first."

"From Ken Gardocki? I haven't heard you mention your gambling debt in a while. Are you doing things for Gardocki?"

"Do you want the money? Because I can get it."

"Did you kill Gardocki's wife?"

"Fuck, Tommy. Why would you ask me something like that?"

"Did you kill Brecht?"

"Tommy, Jesus . . ." He is staring at me with the look of a grade
school teacher who feels you have done something wrong, like he
is going to give me a lecture. He has just received the possibility
of a second layoff in a year. He and his wife and daughter are about
to lose their house and car and wind up in the street and he is worried about whether or not his best friend shot the man who was
going to fire him. I find his morality suddenly ludicrous.

"Yeah, Tommy," I snap. "I fucking shot them. I fucking shot them
both. Fuck them. She was a money-grubbing cheating whore and
he was just an asshole. You know what else? He was going to fire
you and bring in a replacement. Because . . ." I realize I am
screaming, but I don't stop. "Because you didn't put Wenke products on the TOP FUCKING SHELF."

Tommy is staring at me still, eyes blank. He lights a cigarette, his
hands shaking slightly. He is going to tell me to leave and never
come back, that we're not friends anymore, that I am never to set
foot in the convenience store again.

"How much did Gardocki pay you? To shoot Corinne?"

"Five grand," I say softly. "Five grand, but most of it went to pay
my gambling debt."

"Fuck," says Tommy in awe, shaking his head in disbelief. He
takes another drag of his cigarette. "Have you killed anyone else?"

I nod.

"Anyone I know?"

"No."

"Wow," he says. "That's some weird shit." I watch his face for
signs of emotion, fury, hate, distrust. He appears to be thinking,
almost detached.

"You still want to own a store with me?" I ask.

Tommy flips the cigarette out. "You're still Jake, right? I guess it
really doesn't change that much. But I want everything in my
name, in case the cops start giving us trouble." He nervously rattles

off more conditions, mostly commonsense financial advice about hiding assets. There is no moral lecture. He finishes with, ". . . and if you can get the money together like you say, I guess we're partners then."

I shake his hand. "Partners."

He starts getting nervous again, chattering about what will happen if the police come looking for me, whether or not he could pass a lie detector test, and I put my hand on his shoulder.

"Tommy, don't worry," I say. "It'll all be fine."

Tommy has all kinds of questions for me, mostly concerning the mechanics of it, where I get the guns, if I need fake identification, et cetera. I answer the questions cheerfully. His lack of surprise is the most intriguing aspect of the whole interrogation. It's like he knew it all along.

"Why would Gardocki pay you to kill Brecht?" Tommy asks, as if he is trying to piece things together.

"He didn't. That was a Jake Skowran special," I tell him. "You should have seen his personnel files on us. We were all getting it, one way or another. He was going to demote you to clerk and cut your pay."

"Because of the Wenke products?"

"Yup."

Tommy flips his cigarette out. "That bastard. I've got a wife and kid."

"I know. It won't be a problem anymore."

Tommy suddenly sees the good side of being on friendly terms with someone who kills people. It's a safe place to be. And now, with Tommy knowing everything, I realize that it's a lot easier to get time off when your boss knows you're a hired killer.

"I have to go to Miami this weekend," I tell Tommy. "I've got some more work coming up. I'll need some time off."

"I'll talk to Jughead," Tommy says. "And see what you can do about getting some cash up front from Gardocki for the store. February first isn't too far off."

I'm at the Gas'n'Go for about an hour when the phone rings.
"Jake?"
"Yeah?"
"It's Ken."
"Hey, how are you?"
"Listen, people are following me. Cops."
A customer comes into the convenience store and starts making himself a cup of coffee. I try to keep my voice down. I'm sure Ken is just getting paranoid because we shot a state trooper. We. I. Whatever.
"I'm sure nobody's following you, Ken," I say soothingly.
"Listen to me, you asshole. They're not even trying to hide. There is an actual cop car fifty yards behind me everywhere I go. I'm calling you from a pay phone at a movie theater. It's the only place I can go to get away from these jack-offs. There's a plain-clothes cop watching the movie with me."
"What movie?" I ask. I'm a huge film buff. Even after all my finances dried up, I always had enough left for a film a week.
Ken ignores me. "I gotta go. I'm just telling you, I think they're going to start picking people up soon. Make sure your shit is together and you've got all the answers."
"Don't worry," I tell him. "They've got nothing."
"They've got nothing," he repeats, but he sounds worried, and glad to hear the reassuring words from me. "Got to get back to the film." He hangs up.
I call Tommy at home. Mel answers the phone, and she is glad to hear from me, and we chat, a few aimless pleasantries about when is the next time I'm coming over for dinner. Then she puts Tommy on.

"What's up, man?" I can hear a TV on in the background.

"Listen, dude," I tell him in a low voice. "Ken Gardocki just called me. The cops are watching him pretty close, and probably me, too. I might need you to relay messages to him, if we need to communicate."

I can hear Tommy making a face, and I know the face. It's the face he makes about anything remotely worrisome, a late delivery, a performance review, the request to be a part of a hired killing. "Okay," he says doubtfully.

"Later, man."

"Later."

I hang up. The customer is waiting with his coffee, looking at me. I wonder if he is a cop. I take his dollar, and watch him get back into a beat-up white pickup with some roofing company's logo on the side. There are ladders on the truck, and there appears to be real roofing equipment in the back. I've seen him before. He's a roofer. I breathe a little easier as he drives off.

But this is how I have to look at people now.

SEVEN

And the next day, it starts.

There is a knock on the door. "Mister Skowran?"

It's ten in the morning. I have just fallen asleep after spending all night at the convenience store. The first few knocks I just pretend I can't hear, then I hear a police radio from a parked car in the street, and I know what's going on right away. I act sleepier than I feel as I blunder over to the door. "Who is it?" I ask grumpily.

"Mister Skowran, open the door, please."

I make a big show of opening the door, and four men barge in, two of them local cops and two of them plainclothes. A fifth and sixth follow.

"What the hell is going on?" I protest, knowing exactly what is going on. "I was just going to bed."

The first man through the door hands me a piece of paper. "We have a warrant to search your apartment. Could you sign here please, that you have read and understand the terms of the warrant?" He hands me a pen.

"Search it for what?" I make a show of rubbing sleep out of my eyes.

"We'd like you to come down to the station and answer a few questions," he tells me.

"What's this about?"

"Please read the warrant."

The cops walk past me and move off to various parts of my apartment, one going into the kitchen, one in the bedroom, one to the bathroom. They come back.

"There's no one else here," one says.

"No shit," I say. "I could have told you that."

"Start the search in the bedroom," the big plainclothes officer says. "Mister Skowran, please put some clothes on and come down to the station with us."

"Am I under arrest?"

"Not yet," he says.

"So I don't have to go?"

"I'd advise it," he says. "I can have these guys search nice or search nasty. If you want to make a big show, we'll tear your place to bits. It's up to you."

"All right, all right. Jesus," I mutter, irritated, and walk back to my bedroom with a uniformed cop, who is going to watch me put my pants on. I reach for some jeans lying on the floor, and he takes them from me, and feels the pockets, to see if I have a weapon concealed in them anywhere. He hands them back to me.

"What're you guys looking for?" I ask, still pretending to be mystified.

"It's in the warrant, sir," says the cop. I hate when people call me sir when what they really mean is "Fuckface." You can tell by their attitude. "Sir" used to be a word to connote respect, but these people sneer it. Bouncers and cops do this a lot.

"Don't call me sir, I work for a living," I tell him. He watches me quietly as I put my watch on.

I turn to face him. "Want my hands behind my back, to cuff me?"

"You're not under arrest, sir," he says.

"Fuckface." I push by him and go out the door with the detective.

In the back of the police car, I look out the window as I see my town go by. Snow drips off broken mailboxes at the end of unpaved driveways. A few houses are boarded up, houses which just a year ago were thriving, kids playing on the lawn. A traffic light has fallen into the street near what used to be a busy intersection. It will still be there a week from now.

I think about what is going on, and I know that I am in command. They've got nothing. If they had anything, they'd arrest me. There's nothing in my apartment to link me to anything, so they can search around all they want. I wonder if Sheila is down at the police station, or if it is her day off. Perhaps after the interrogation I'll ask her to lunch. Or maybe I'll just go back to bed.

This time, the cops are ready to interrogate me and they have an interrogation room set up, awaiting me. No waiting around now. I see Detective Martz, big and burly in his pressed white shirt, and I nod hello to him as I sit in The Chair, and he ignores my pleasantry. He opens a folder as two other detectives sit on either side of him.

It starts quickly.

Martz throws me a picture of Karl. "Do you know this man?"

"Yeah. This is Karl."

"Where is he?"

"I don't know."

"How do you know him?"

"From around."

"Around what?" asks Martz.

"Did you guys hang out? Were you friends?" asks another detective.

"When was the last time you saw him?" asks the third. So this is how it's going to be. The Question Barrage Technique. I've seen too many TV shows, documentaries about police work, mostly on the Discovery Channel before they took my cable away, to find anything they do surprising. I look calmly from one to the other.

"Let's go one at a time," I say politely.

They all start asking me questions again. They have taken my request as a sign that their Question Barrage has me rattled, so they're going to keep it up until I explode in a fit of rage and truth. *Yes! Yes! I killed Karl! He's in a ditch somewhere off Route 27! Just stop with the simultaneous questions!* I shake my head and stare at them. I look at Martz.

"I know him from around the neighborhood," I tell him. I focus on Martz and only Martz, and imagine I can't hear or see the other two detectives.

All three of them ask me some more questions, but I focus only on Martz, who asks, "Do you know a man named Ken Gardocki?"

"Of course I know him," I say.

"Why of course?"

I shrug. Why of course? Did I give something away? "I've known him for years," I say.

"Do you know about his business practices?" Martz asks. The other detectives have become quiet. This is Technique Number Two, pretending they're primarily interested in someone else in the hopes that I'll become more forthcoming. People are more willing to open up when discussing a third party. Thank you, Discovery Channel's *The Prosecutors*.

"I've heard rumors."

"Are you aware he runs a gambling operation?"

I smile, laugh even. They assume that it is from relief, that I am finally understanding this is not about any of the murders I have committed, but about small-time stuff, in the hopes that I will open up more. "I sure am," I nod.

"Have you ever placed a bet with Mr. Gardocki?"

"Yes," I say.

"Are you aware that gambling is illegal in the state of Wisconsin?"

"Yes," I say.

"So you're admitting to a felony," says Martz.

"It's only illegal if you get paid money," I say. "We were doing it for points."

"Points?" Martz looks at me long and hard, the Intimidating Stare I've seen on *The New Detectives*. "What do you win when you've got enough 'points?'" He says the last word with disdain, as if it's the most ridiculous thing he's ever heard.

"A mountain bike," I say.

I'm making this up as I go along now, just enjoying myself. Why am I here? Yes, okay, I've shot some people. But is this really the top priority of the local government right now, that they can afford all this manpower, to try to find a reason to put me in a cage and feed me for the rest of my life? They made me an animal, and now they want to treat me like one?

Martz realizes this line of questioning is going nowhere. He plucks a single sheet of paper out of a file. "Mr. Skowran, did you ever place a bet on a game between the Buffalo Bills and the New York Jets?"

"I've bet on a lot of games. I would imagine I did."

"Who won that game?"

"Are you kidding? I need a date. I can't remember every game I ever bet on."

Martz sits back, looking victorious. "I would think you'd remember that game," he says slowly. "Because you won five thousand, eight hundred . . . points." He throws me the piece of paper, which is one of Ken Gardocki's betting sheets. On it is written "JSK (which I assume is Gardocki's code-name for me) BUF-NYJ-out 5,800." It could mean anything. Okay, though, I won't argue this. They've obviously cracked Gardocki's betting codes.

"Surely that's enough points for your mountain bike," Martz says. "And you don't remember who won? You don't remember the game that won you your mountain bike?"

I start to say something. The momentum is slipping over to Martz. He's good. They don't mention on *The FBI Files* how much all these psychological tricks wear on you over time. That's why these interrogations go on for hours, and this is just the first few minutes. This is going to be a long day.

Martz interrupts me. "I know if I won fifty-eight hundred . . . *points* . . . I'd remember everything about the game that won me that money. I'd remember every pass, every third down play. Unless, of course, there wasn't really a bet. Unless of course, someone *gave* me the money to do them a favor, like say, kill his wife."

Wow. These guys have figured out a lot. The betting sheet thing hasn't tripped them up a bit. There is a silence in the room.

"The Jets won," I say finally. "24-21. A field goal in the final three minutes, which they had to kick twice because the first one was called back on a penalty. Testaverde went 12 of 19 for 233 yards, two TDs and no interceptions." I have done my homework. "I can go quarter by quarter, if you'd like."

This goes on and on. They spring one thing on me after another. They know Brecht and Corinne Gardocki were shot with the same gun. They know Brecht was my boss. They know Corinne Gardocki was the wife of a man to whom I owed a lot of money. They know Karl knew me. They know he's disappeared. But I dance. Because basically, they don't *know* anything. All they've done is draw a lot of astute conclusions and they have absolutely no evidence to back any of it up. I sure do look guilty on paper, but they haven't got enough to charge me or they'd just do it.

After about two hours, a fourth detective comes in and whispers in Martz' ear for a few seconds. Martz looks at me, and I get a brief chill. They've found something. Maybe Karl's body.

Martz leans back. Stares at me thoughtfully. Technique number . . . What number are we up to now? It's got to be in the low thirties. The longer he stares, the less alarmed I feel. He's dragging it out too long.

"You had seventy-two hundred in cash in your apartment," he says.

"Yes," I say quickly. "That's my money."

"That's a lot of cash, isn't it?"

"It's quite a bit," I say cheerfully. It suddenly occurs to me that they are going to take it. Fuck. Now I'm broke again.

"Where did you get it?'

"I earned it, back when I was at the factory."

"You had all this money, yet you let them repo your car? You let them cut off your cable?" He pushes copies of my credit card bills towards me. "You never paid a credit card bill?"

"Is it illegal to not pay your bills? Is that why I'm here?" Martz stares at me. For two more hours this goes on. For two more hours, I dance.

I go home, and my place is ransacked. The cops have torn everything apart. I thought they were going to search "nice." Isn't that what I was promised? I've got hours upon hours of clean-up ahead of me. Being a hired killer has its down side.

I curl up in bed, the adrenaline from the interrogation wearing off. I was good. I didn't crack. I didn't slip. I have a talent here.

I finally get some sleep, after a hard day's work.

                                    * * *

"Jake," Ken Gardocki tells me as I pull a six-pack from the cooler in the back of his SUV. "I want you to kill the guy who fucked my wife."

"Sure, dude. No problem." I tear a beer out of the six-pack and hand it to him as we head out onto the ice with our deck chairs. "Where and when?"

It has been two days since the interrogation, since the cops stole my money for "evidence." I had to go over and see Gardocki to see if he could provide me with living expenses for the next few days. I thought he would be horrified to see me in his office, go off on a paranoid rant about "them watching us," but when he opened the door he just smiled and welcomed me in. He gave me three hundred-dollar bills and suggested we go fishing out on Bear Lake.

The cops had a warrant for Gardocki, too, and apart from a mention of a mountain bike, our stories had matched perfectly. They had interrogated us at the same time, had trashed his office just like they did my apartment. But Gardocki, with years of criminal ventures under his belt, had squirreled his money away somewhere else. When I told him about the confiscation of my newfound wealth, he just waved his hand and made a face as if to say, "I hate when that happens."

"Miami," Gardocki says as he kneels down and starts chipping away at the ice. We are several hundred yards away from the ice shack, where there is a hole already drilled in the ice, but Gardocki isn't going anywhere near it because he is afraid of bugging devices. We don't talk about anything in his office, in his car, in any building he frequents, not even the Bar in the Middle of Nowhere. Especially not there. Gardocki had been fishing in that shack a few weeks ago, so now we stand outside on the ice, and he cuts a new hole.

"I hear Miami's nice this time of year," I say.

"I think it would be best if you brought someone with you," he says. "You know, like a girl."

"A girl?"

"Yeah. You know a girl, don't you?"

"I know a few. I'm not sure any of them want to go to Miami with me."

Gardocki laughs. "Just ask nice. You're a good-looking guy. Free plane ticket, a couple of days in the sun. Who'd say no to that?"

Who'd say no? Lots of people. I've hardly had an hour's worth of conversation with women since Kelly left. My anger at the layoffs and my anger at Kelly's almost clinical, immediate abandonment of me merged into a single fury at the world, at women, relationships, procreation, the survival of the species. I didn't care about anything, anyone. The hit-man career has relieved some of the anger, and I'm feeling some interest again. But I hardly want to be asking anyone to fly off to Miami with me for days on end. I'm hardly sure if I even want to spend three days with anyone.

"I think I'd be better off by myself," I tell Gardocki.

"Are you nuts? They're watching everything you do. They're watching me. They're going to trace the plane ticket, and realize I bought it. Then they're going to see you went to Miami on your own, stayed three days, and some guy in a hotel died when you were there. Jesus, Jake, they've got enough circumstantial evidence as it is. You can't keep making mountain-bike jokes to these guys forever, they're serious." He pauses. "But if you had a woman there, it wouldn't be so circumstantial, would it? You could just say I lent you guys money to go down there for a vacation, because your credit's bad right now."

"I'm working on that," I say, shivering.

"I don't give a shit about your credit," Gardocki says. "You're missing the point. I'll take care of everything, hotel reservations and all that shit, and this way it doesn't look funny. You can't do it because of your credit cards. They know we know each other. But if there's no cover story for you being down there, the dead pilot looks extra fishy, especially if they tie him to Corinne."

His argument makes sense. I do need a woman. I'm going to have to ask one. My new line of work is forcing me out of the hermit-like existence, out of the cocoon I have wrapped around myself since the layoffs. I'm going to have to ask a woman out on a three-day date, and so far I haven't even got a woman who I know will go out with me for an evening.

"Ken, honestly, I don't know any women. I haven't been socializing a lot lately."

Gardocki gives me a cold look. "What's the matter with you? Just get a woman. It's fucking Miami, three days in a three-star hotel. Anyone you ask'll say yes. Take someone married, I don't give a shit." He reaches into his pocket and pulls out an envelope full of money and hands it to me. "Spend some of this on her first, warm her up."

Out on the lake, the sun is going down and Gardocki and I are sitting in deck chairs pretending we are ice fishing, getting good and drunk. I pull the tab off another six pack and hand him a beer. He has been describing how I'm going to do the job, and this time I don't think his plan is very good.

"It's only about two hundred yards," Gardocki tells me. "It'll be easy."

"I've never fired a rifle, Ken. Did you see *Saving Private Ryan?* I don't think being a sniper looked all that easy."

He shrugs. "That was a war movie. People were trying to kill him. This is just you, sitting on a roof, drawing a bead on an unsuspecting guy." He's already convinced this is going to be a cinch, that I just need to boost my confidence and get on with it, like asking out a woman. "It'll be six a.m. He'll be in the water, and there won't be anyone else around. He goes for a swim in the sea every time he's in Miami, at six. Hell, you can miss a few times. The farther out he is when you get him, the better off you'll be. Maybe an undertow will get his body and they won't find him for days, and they'll think he drowned."

"Then they'll notice half his head is missing . . ."

Gardocki laughs. "Maybe they'll think a shark took it."

Gardocki laughs because he thinks I am invincible, that the minute I set my mind to do this, it'll be a great success. I've done right by him so far, killed his wife, protected him from Karl, all without getting us in trouble. Not any trouble which can guarantee a conviction, at any rate. He thinks I have some magical gift, when in fact, it has been mostly luck. My crimes to date have been free of witnesses. But now Gardocki thinks that I have mad hit-man skills, that any method of murder he came up with would just be a breeze for me. As if he could knowingly hand me a garrote, a knife, a Claymore mine, and I would set to work with skills I've been concealing for all those years when I was disguising myself as a loading dock manager. The fact is, once I get away from the old pistol-from-two-yards-away method that I've perfected, I have no idea what I'm doing.

"Give it a try," he says. He has a satisfied look in his eye, and I know that he really wants this man to die this way. Being shot by a paid sniper while going for a swim is the type of death a man of power orders. It is a political assassination, a covert hit. It just seems like a bunch of bullshit to me. Dead is dead.

"She was going to kill me, Jake," Gardocki says, as he gazes across the frozen lake. "Corinne and that pilot, they had a plan. She was going to kill me and move to Florida. They'd even picked out a house, in Miami."

"Come on, Ken. How do you know that?"

"I'd read her e-mails. I used to pretend that I didn't know how to use a computer, and I didn't want to learn. I'd never even turn the thing on. She felt safe e-mailing the guy. I'm a bookie, for Chrissake, I use a computer all the time. I can practically program one. So one day, I got a hold of her password and read some of her e-mails. They were coded, sure, but it wasn't difficult to see it was about killing me. Sometimes it wasn't even coded. They were going to make it look like a burglar did it one night when I was home, after I got back from Denver."

"Jesus," I say. I try to imagine what it must be like to find out your wife of ten years is planning to kill you, imagine Gardocki's shock as he opened the files on her computer, his expression as he read each word and put together their significance. "That's gotta suck."

Gardocki shrugs. "Hey, I married a stripper twenty years younger than me. You gotta be careful. You know something, though?"

"What?"

"She was a terrible stripper." Gardocki laughs at the memory. "Man, that girl couldn't dance for shit. That was why I liked her, because she just didn't seem to belong there." His eyes glaze over a little and he finishes his beer, throws the empty can on the ice and we watch it skid for a while, then come to a stop. "You did me a real favor, Jake. You did a good job. That was a great service you did me." He pats his leg awkwardly, not wanting to suffer a spell of beer-induced emotion, which I feel coming on. They should make beer commercials about conversations like this. Show a logo saying "To Good Friends" and then show Gardocki, thanking me so sincerely for killing his wife in a timely and professional manner, as he takes another swig and then holds the beer up to the camera.

"But my point is," he says, suddenly aware he is getting emotional. "I want this fucker's brains blown out while he is taking a dip in the sea. Sound good?"

"I'll see what I can do."

I do take advantage of the situation, though.

While Gardocki is getting lit up, and I am starting to feel a nice rush myself, I bring up the subject of him lending me and Tommy the money to buy the Gas'n'Go. I squeeze it in at just the right time, between the gratitude and the planning of the actual killing, when the sincere compliments have not yet worn off.

"What the fuck you guys want to buy that dinky little place for?" he laughs.

"It's not so dinky. It grosses about a hundred eighty thousand a year. After stock and wages, that'll leave about thirty grand each for Tommy and me."

"Thirty grand a year ain't much," he says. "How're you guys going to pay me back forty grand out of sixty grand? That means you'll only make ten grand a year each the first year."

Gardocki is, was and always will be a businessman. "We'll only owe you thirty grand, because you're giving me ten to do this guy in Miami. Do we have to pay you back everything the first year?" I can be a businessman, too, when I have to. The price for the Miami killing has never been discussed.

"That's normally the way I do it," he says. He shakes his head. "I don't like to lend money like that. That's a lot of money."

Dammit, what happened to the I-love-you-Jake phase we were just entering? I guess he wasn't as drunk or as sincere as I thought. There is something shaming about asking for money, and now I can't even look at him anymore. I stare down at my feet as Gardocki opens a bag of sunflower seeds and starts popping them in his mouth, then spitting the hulls onto the ice.

"Tell you what, though," he says. "Why don't you two get a business loan from the bank, and I'll co-sign."

I brighten up immediately. "You would?" I haven't heard that much hope in my own voice in months. It spreads through my whole body, giving me energy I didn't know was there anymore, making me want to jump up and sing. I sit upright in my deck chair and ask again. "You really would?"

"Sure," Gardocki nods. "You'd have to make the payments on time, though, or it'd be my ass."

"We'll make the payments," I tell him. I start babbling about how I'll never miss a payment, about how they used to call me Reliable Jake or some shit like that when I was working at the factory, about how I'm obviously used to living on next to nothing, thanks to the layoffs. I'm like an economic cockroach, I can survive anything. Gardocki isn't listening. He's chuckling.

"Convenience store," he says, shaking his head. "What the fuck's the matter with you two guys?"

Tulley's is hopping. There are at least twenty people inside, twenty-one if you count Tony Wolek, who is running around, gray-faced, popping the tops of beers as fast as he can pull them out of the coolers. He sees me come in and plops a beer down in front of me without looking at me, then gets back to the "crowd." It used to be like this every night, but Tony is out of practice.

"Nice crowd you got here tonight," I tell him when he gets a calm moment.

"Darts tournament finals," he says.

I get right to the point. "Do you know a girl named Sheila who plays in that tournament? She's a cop, works downtown."

"She's not a cop," Tony tells me. "She works for the police department but she doesn't carry a gun." Tony has all the info on everyone, like the shoeshine guy in an old detective novel. He knows why I'm asking, too. "She lives with her boyfriend," he tells me.

"Things good between 'em?"

Tony smiles, an expression I haven't seen from him in some time. "What're you planning, Jake?" Some more people come up to the bar and Tony runs off, makes some drinks. Then he comes back and says, "I don't think so."

Talking with Tony when his bar is busy is always like this, three-minute time delays between the questions and the answers, and now I've forgotten what the question was. I was watching the highlights of the Red Wings game. Then I remember I'd been asking about Sheila, and whether she was getting along with her boyfriend.

"He's a big guy," Tony warns me.

And I'm a murdering maniac. At least, according to Ken Gardocki.

Tony leans on the bar and looks me straight in the eye. "He's a truck driver," he tells me. "He's away all the time. She's pissed about that, thinking about moving out. She also thinks he cheats on her when he's on the road. A little while back she got some kind of infection from him."

"Jesus, what've you got, surveillance equipment set up in their bedroom?"

Tony smiles again, shrugs. "She was in here about two weeks ago with her girlfriends. One of 'em had a birthday. They were here all night. You hear stuff."

I wonder how much he's heard from me. Have I ever said anything while I was sitting at the bar that I wouldn't want the world to know? Up until recently, I didn't have any secrets at all.

"And," Tony says, as if saving the most important detail for last, "He's a shitty tipper."

I'm in. Tony, at least, is on my side.

I watch the Red Wings highlights so many times I start to feel like I went to the game. Sheila's darts team is getting pasted, but she is nowhere around. They're playing without her. I wonder what could possibly be keeping her from an all-important, crucial event like this. An argument with her boyfriend? A broken-down car? Emergency cop business? I down another beer and consider calling it a night. A few more of these and I won't be able to pronounce Miami, let alone ask someone to accompany me there.

I start thinking about back-up possibilities. Tommy could lend me Mel for the weekend. I don't know how happy he'd be about that, but hey, he wants a convenience store as much as I do. I'd have to promise to keep my hands off her, of course, but the real promising would have to be Mel's. I've heard things about her over the years. No proof of anything, just rumor, but I'm sure there is something to it. She gives me long looks sometimes when I'm over at Tommy's house, leans over a little too far in loose-fitting shirts when she's handing me a beer. I was always willing to let it go because Tommy is my best friend, but guys like Zorda, you never know. I start distracting myself with thoughts of what she looks like naked, what kind of noises she'd make as I fucked her senseless in a Miami hotel room with the windows open and a gentle breeze rustling the hotel drapes. Screams? No . . . My guess is she's lived too many years with a small child in the house to be a screamer any more. Muffled gasps, more like, deep throaty moans which . . .

"Hi." I feel a hand on my back and jerk backwards. I hold onto my beer but manage to throw half of it onto my shirt. Even as I'm doing this, I recognize Sheila's perfume and raspy voice, and before the last of the beer has even splashed into my chest I've already asked myself about a dozen questions. What does the light touch on my back mean? Why does she come over and say hi to me before going over and talking to her darts team?

"Aaaah," she yells, laughing. "I'm sorry. I didn't mean to sneak up on you." She takes the seat next to me and grabs me a bar napkin, and before I can take it from her, she starts wiping my shirt. I tighten my chest muscles to make sure it feels firm, and I have an immediate idea that she's noticed that vain effort. I lean in a little to get a nice whiff of whatever she is wearing, a nice, subtle perfume. I can feel the cold from the outside on her skin and jacket, and it is exhilarating, sexy. She doesn't lean back.

"I'm sorry," she says again in her raspy voice, giving my chest a final wipe. Tony comes over and puts two beers down in front of us, my usual Budweiser and a local Milwaukee brew for her.

"That's on this guy," Tony says pointing to me. Good ole Tony, trying to help me out here.

"No, Tony," she says. "Put them on me. I just made him spill it."

"Thanks," I say.

She laughs again. "So," she asks, her voice still full of fun. "What'd you do?"

"What did I do?"

"Yeah. Why'd the cops want to talk to you?"

"Oh, yeah, that." I remember now that the last time I saw her was when Detective Martz was leading me away for questioning. I am momentarily stuck for an explanation. I've worked out everything necessary to say to the police when questioned, but those answers don't wash in a personal context. To the cops, I'd say, "Nothing . . . I did absolutely nothing." But to a girl I want to date, I need something else. Treating an innocent question like a police interrogation probably isn't going to get me very far with this woman, and I want to keep the conversation moving smoothly. Admitting to several killings will probably stop the conversation dead in its tracks, as will telling her to mind her own business. I need something middle-of-the-road.

"Parking tickets," I say quickly. "I've been having a hell of a time with 'em."

She smiles knowingly as she looks at her beer. "That would be the Admin Building across the street," she says.

That's the second time I've been busted in the same lie, I realize. I laugh. She knows I've done something and she likes watching me wriggle around. Blame Ken Gardocki, my brain suddenly says.

"Do you know a guy named Ken Gardocki?" I ask.

"Yeah. I dated him."

Wow. This is news. How small is this town? I'm left speechless by this piece of information, as well as noticing an opportunity to change the subject. "You dated Ken Gardocki?"

"Yeah." She shrugs. "About ten years ago, for maybe a month. Just after his wife died. I felt sorry for him." She realizes this has had more effect on me than she intended, and she downplays it with a wave of her hand. "No big deal," she says. "So . . . were you dealing drugs for Gardocki?"

"Oh, hell no," I say quickly, but am subtly aware, even as I deny it, that the opposite answer would have had a beneficial effect as a device to impress her. She likes bad boys, I realize suddenly. "I try to stay out of the drug scene these days," I say, downplaying my denial. "I stick more with the gambling side of things."

She nods. She knows of Gardocki's business practices. "So what do you do? You a leg breaker?" She takes a swig of beer and looks at me directly, the hard direct stare that so aroused me last time I met her here.

I'm going to go along with this, while trying to tell as few actual lies as possible. What could be more intriguing to a girl who likes bad boys than meeting an enforcer for a local mobster? "Leg breaking isn't my thing," I tell her. "Usually I just discuss. Act as his spokesman-on-the-street." There, I've made myself sound like the intellectual, caring mobster that all women want.

"So you don't actually beat people up?"

I don't want to disappoint her with another denial, so I switch the subject. "Let's talk about you," I say, and this attempt to change the subject seems to have charmed her all the more. If I'm trying to wriggle away from a conversation, then there must be a reason for the wriggling. I've created a sense of mystery about myself while admitting to nothing. Maybe I do beat people up, maybe not. Good move, Jake.

"What about me?" She leans back and starts to remove her black leather jacket, and I notice large, firm breasts being pointed forward as she shrugs the jacket off. I try to look subtly, and am probably not as subtle as I think. She knows where my attention is and I have the idea she is slowing the whole jacket removal process down for my benefit. She hangs the jacket over the back of her chair and shakes out her hair, then looks at me.

"Do you have to work tomorrow?" I ask.

"No. I'm off until Tuesday. I have to take my cat to the vet, though." She is still looking at me intensely, as if trying to read all kinds of information. Am I violent, unpredictable, kind? What do I want from her? Love, sex, passion, someone to dominate and abuse?

"Do you want to go to Miami for the weekend?"

She laughs. I can't believe I just blurted that out, feel some need to take it back, apologize for being so forward, but before I can say anything else, she says, "I'd love to go to Miami for the weekend. Wouldn't that be nice?"

I realize she thinks that it was just a fantasy question. "It would be nice," I say. And then, to bring her around to the idea that it's not a joke, I add, "I actually have an extra ticket."

"You're serious?" She looks more curious than alarmed. To my surprise, she seems to be thinking about it, or perhaps she's just looking for a way out. "I don't even know you," she says.

"It'd be a perfect opportunity for us to get to know each other." Oooh, smooth. I like that. But it was too smooth. She seems to have lost interest in the conversation. She glances over at the darts game.

"I'm supposed to be playing darts," she says. "I've missed almost the whole game. They're going to be mad."

"How come you were late?"

She turns back to me and tells me a quick story about her ailing cat, who apparently had vomited all over her apartment. But she has become restless now, the flirtation has stopped. "So I have to take my cat to the vet," she finishes. "I'm sorry, I won't be able to act as your cover while you go on a drug run for Ken Gardocki." She hops out of her chair.

"This has nothing to do with drugs," I say as she walks away. "I told you . . . I don't do that. It's just a vacation."

But she goes over to her darts partners. She doesn't look back.

"That went well," Tony says. "Another beer?"

"Nah." I pay my tab and get up to leave.

"Hey," Tony calls after me. "Don't give up. You never know."

"Fuck it."

On the way home, I think about things.

Mel is still a possibility, but I don't want to bother with it. I've been without a woman for too long to realistically expect myself to push her away if she makes any advance at all, and I don't want my partnership with Tommy to be soured from the beginning by the notion that I've fucked his wife. Sheila's a goner. Maybe Denise, from the debt-collection service? I get mail from them.

They're located in Buffalo, New York. Who needs a weekend in Miami this time of year more than those people? Maybe I could promise to pay my debts in full, plus late fees and interest charges, if she came to Miami with me and let me bang her like a Turkish sailor on a three-day pass in an Asian port.

Maybe not.

Then there's Kelly. If I called her and told her to pack her things for the weekend, she'd think it was some kind of desperate attempt to reconcile, not a desperate attempt to get an accomplice who'd make me less suspicious come my next homicide interrogation. Besides, I spent eight years with her, eight years based on trust. I couldn't very well put her in that situation, despite how angry her abandonment made me. Maybe one day I'll open that letter she sent me.

When Gardocki mentioned that it would be easy for me to find a woman at short notice, I think he had some fantasy notion of my life. Maybe he imagined that a laid-off factory employee just spent his whole time going to parties and meeting people, turning his endless free time into a chance to pursue social engagements. Retirement may well be like that for him. But there's a psychological toll which he didn't take into account. If your company tells you you're not wanted, you assume nobody wants you. Despite my endless free time, I found myself withdrawing from people, not even willing to make eye contact with the librarian when I checked out books. I turned down social invitations so frequently that I stopped getting them. And I know I'm not the only one.

Being a hired killer was just so much easier when I could do it alone.

EIGHT

I'm picking up my CDs, which the cops have thrown all over the floor despite their promise to "search nice" if I didn't cause a scene, when the phone rings. It is Gardocki, calling from a pay phone. I'd asked Tommy to call him to tell him to call me, though after thinking about it, I really should just have called him myself. It's legal for me to talk to Gardocki.

"Meet me at the place," he says, and hangs up.

The Place? Is that a new restaurant? His codes are good. Good enough to fool the people who are expected to understand them. But I figure he means the bar where Karl used to drive me, so I hop in my car and drive forty-five minutes into the woods to find out it is closed and the parking lot is empty. Where else could "The Place" be? That restaurant where he bought me an Italian meal ages ago, the day he told me about the plan to kill Corinne? God, that's over an hour in the other direction. I'm running low on gas, so when I get back into town I swing by the convenience store to fill up.

Tommy is there. "Where the hell you been?" he asks when I walk in to pay for the gas.

"Why?"

"Ken Gardocki was here for over an hour, waiting for you. He went back to his office." So the Gas'n'Go was "The Place." What's the point of that? How silly has this whole code-word thing become? The Gas'n'Go is where I work. The cops know where I work. If Gardocki wants to have a secret meeting with me, how secret would it be if we do it in broad daylight at my job? And if it doesn't need to be secret, why not just say "I'll meet you at the convenience store?" The cops know that Ken Gardocki and I spend time together, for whatever reason. This is like wiping your fingerprints off something you own.

"What's the matter with him?" I ask.

"He was asking me that about you."

"He thinks there's something wrong with both of us for wanting to own this store."

Tommy looks apprehensive. "Do you really think he'll lend us the money?"

"Oh, yeah."

Tommy's cheeks are flushed with enthusiasm, and his smile is shining. It's not an expression I see often around here. Over a crappy little convenience store. But we found a way out. We are going to survive.

"He mentioned something about wanting to send Mel down to Miami with you," Tommy says, opening the register and counting change. "I told him she'd love it. But I'd have to close the store to look after Jenny, so I don't see how we could do it."

This is getting too weird. Tommy is willing to let me take his wife to a romantic vacation spot so that I can kill someone. But it isn't concern over his wife's fidelity that is holding him back, or morality. It's his inability to find a sitter.

"Tell Gardocki to mind his own business," I say. "I think I'm just going to go by myself. That's what I wanted to tell him."

"He's in his office. Tell him yourself."

I drive up to Gardocki's office, where he is alarmed to see me. He puts his forefinger over his lips as if to shush me, then madly scribbles something on a piece of paper and hands it to me. THIS OFFICE MIGHT BE BUGGED.

I write something and hand the paper back. NO WOMAN FOR MIAMI.

He rolls his eyes, looks at me and shrugs, as if to say, "What's the matter with you?"

He scribbles I ASKED TOMMY ABOUT HIS WIFE. SHE'LL GO. DON'T WANT TO.

FUCK, JAKE. IT'S BUSINESS. YOU HAVE TO.

RATHER GO ALONE.

NO NO NO. A lot of head of head-shaking accompanies this one. MAYBE NEXT MONTH. NEED TIME.

ALREADY BOUGHT TICKETS. NON-REFUNDABLE. TOMMY'S WIFE. Underlined about three times. He doesn't even know Mel's name, but he smiles as he adds SHE'S NOT BAD LOOKING.

I snatch the piece of paper from him and ball it up, throw it on his desk, shaking my head furiously. "NO!" I yell and storm out. I expect him to follow me and start yelling, but I get into my car to drive off and I notice the door to his office is still closed. He understands. He knows I'm right about this. He can take the damned money for the tickets out of my payment, if he likes, but I'm not putting myself in a situation where I might fuck my best friend's wife.

I get home and there is a strange car in my driveway. Shit! The cops have come back to dump my CDs everywhere again. I look at the

car, and realize it is too old to be a cop car, and I see Sheila standing at my front door. She is writing a note.

"Hey," she says, crumpling the note and putting it in her pocket.

"Hey, how are you?"

She doesn't say anything.

"What's up?"

"I've been thinking." That voice again. I'd marry her for the
voice alone. Deep, sexy and confident.

"About what?"

"You still want me to go to Miami?"

I try to be Cool Jake, but I find myself breaking into a smile.
"Hell, yeah. You wanna go?"

She steps back, slightly intimidated by my enthusiasm. "Listen,
Jake," she says. "All I want is a vacation. I know you're doing some
stuff for Gardocki, and I don't care what it is, but I'm not putting
any drugs in my suitcase or stuff like that. I just want to get out of
here for a few days."

"No problem."

"And we get separate rooms in the hotel."

"No. Can't do that." Shit. "If you go, we have to share a room."
What kind of girlfriend can I claim she is if we have separate rooms?
"Separate beds is fine. Hell, if there's only one bed, I'll sleep on the
floor, I don't care." Actually, I do care, but business is business. She
already knows she's being used as cover, so I don't have to sweet-
talk her. I need to stop thinking about getting laid for a second and
concentrate on the job at hand. "It'll be great," I tell her. "The flight's
tomorrow at nine thirty. I promise to be a perfect gentleman."

She gives this some thought. "You can't tell anyone from here
that I'm going with you. I live with someone."

"I know. That's no problem, either."

"You know?"

I shrug.

"What's going on with you? Did you do, like, a background
check on me?"

"No. I asked Tony at the bar."

She gives this some thought. "That's okay," she says finally. "I asked him about you, too."

"Really? What'd he say about me?"

Now it's her turn to shrug. She looks at me intently. "You're not going to put drugs in my suitcase?"

I laugh. "I told you, I don't do that. I don't have anything to do with drugs."

She doesn't look convinced. With a wary expression, she gets back in her car.

"Hey," I call after her. "How's your cat?"

She waves the question off and screeches off out of the driveway, spraying snow against my legs. I run up the stairs, almost giddy with excitement, and call Gardocki.

"The problem is solved," I tell him.

I know he is dying of curiosity, but all he can say is "Good." He hangs up. Yeeeehaaaaaa! I'm one happy hit man.

During the flight down, Sheila is quiet, careful not to be too flirtatious, worried about giving me the wrong idea. She orders a beer on the plane even though it is only ten in the morning. Maybe flying is making her nervous. Maybe I'm making her nervous. Maybe she drinks at ten in the morning all the time.

"I didn't tell my boyfriend about this trip," she says, staring at the back of the seat in front of her.

What am I supposed to say to that? Why is she telling me this? Does she want to talk about her boyfriend? "What's he like?" I ask.

"He's okay."

Not exactly a ringing endorsement. She keeps staring at the seat cover like she's expecting a vision of Jesus to appear in it. I hope she relaxes a little when we get there. Right now, I can just feel the anxiety radiating from her, can almost hear her telling herself this wasn't such a good idea.

"When we get to the hotel, I have to go run an errand," I tell her. "You can go for a swim or something, then we can go out to dinner, if you'd like."

"Okay." Still staring at the seat cover.

"Great, then."

"This is weird," she says. She turns to me. "Do you think this is weird?"

"No. Why, because you only just met me?"

"Yeah."

"It's not weird."

This seems to cheer her up. "You don't think so?"

"No."

"I think it's weird."

She's lying to her boyfriend about flying off to Miami with someone she doesn't know, to act as his cover while he commits a crime of some kind. What's weird about that? Happens all the time. All I know is, I'm having a good time. This is a hell of a lot more fun than sitting in my snow-bound apartment waiting for the mailman to bring me unemployment checks. I take her hand. "Thanks for coming down," I say. "I appreciate it."

She takes her eyes off the seat cover and looks at me (finally). She takes her hand back and says nothing.

The car Gardocki has rented for me is an old Nissan Sentra, the cheap bastard. The people at the airport rental office just shake their heads when I tell them it is supposed to be a Chrysler Sebring convertible. I only know they have such a convertible because I saw it through the fence on my way in from the arrival gate, and I figure I'll try having a shot at pretending Gardocki made a mistake. On the flight down I've imagined Sheila and myself soaring along a coastal highway in a convertible, the wind blowing through her hair. Stupid. A bunch of rental agents all gather around me and start asking me questions about how such a mistake could possibly have happened, and I realize that I have just committed the ultimate hitman sin: I've made people notice me. A good hired killer, like a

good baseball umpire, needs to make sure he fades into the woodwork.

"It says mini-compact," the man behind the counter says with
the nervous tone of someone who doesn't want his credibility
questioned.

"Can you upgrade it?"

"We'd need to have authorization from the person whose name
is on the credit card," he says. "A Mr. Ken Gar . . . Gar . . . ."

"Gardocki, yeah." I can tell this guy has had this conversation
before. Apparently, a lot of businessmen come down here with fan-
tasies of wind blowing through their hair and then realize their
bosses are cheap bastards. "I can give you cash for the difference,"
I tell him.

"We can't do that," he says, almost alarmed, shaking his head, as
if I've threatened to steal the Sebring. His fear and nervousness and
obsession with paperwork are making me annoyed.

"Why the hell not?"

He looks flustered, then runs back into an office and comes out
with an even more ferrety-looking guy, who I assume is his manager. "That's the car that was reserved for you," the manager says.
"That's all we have right now." He walks back into his office.

That was pretty rude, I'm thinking to myself. Sheila comes up
behind me and puts her hand gently on my back. "What's going
on?" she asks.

"I want to rent a Sebring, and they won't let me," I tell her.

"It's not that we won't let you," says the counter guy. "It's just that
we don't have it right now." He looks at Sheila and says soothingly,
"If you come back tomorrow, I can arrange for you to have it at the
same price."

She smiles at him and thanks him, and puts her arm around me.
"Let's come back here tomorrow," she says. I know damned well
that the Sebring isn't going anywhere today, that the counter guy
just doesn't like me and he's fucking with me because he can. I
remember doing things like that to people who were rude to me

when I was managing the dock. "Oh, no sir, we can't get those track replacement tabs out to you today . . . If I put a rush on it, I can have it to you by Thursday," as I sat with my feet up on a crate of track replacement tabs, while a truck driver going to this guy's store was about to leave. That's what you got for screaming "fuck" at me earlier in the conversation. Perhaps next time he'd have more manners. I can tell this guy feels the same way. Doesn't like my attitude. I had forgotten that important lesson. But a flirtatious smile from Sheila has defused him, and an arm around me has defused me. She's good.

The little bastard hands me my paperwork without looking at me. Sheila smiles at him again and thanks him.

"You have a nice day," he says to her, as if I'm not there.

The car's muffler is about to fall off, and it makes more noise than a motorcycle as I pull into the hotel parking lot. We are right on the beach, but we are NEXT DOOR to the hotel where the pilot is staying, I realize. Gardocki is going to tell me that it is better, if anyone investigates, not to have our names on the same hotel register, though now that I can see both hotels, I realize that economic concerns might have entered into his thinking.

The pilot's hotel, the Ambassador, is a soaring ten-story affair that looks like new construction. My hotel is a dinky little two-story shit hole. It looks like it was picked up, in one piece, from a plot of land across from a truck stop in Oklahoma and dropped here right on the Miami beachfront. Judging by the giant neon sign, the place is apparently called *Vacancy*, a status which is immediately understandable.

Sheila isn't disappointed, which makes me like her all the more. She's just happy to be out of Wisconsin, away from snow, happy to be near a beach in the sunshine. The old car, the crappy hotel, it's fine. "I wasn't planning to spend much time here anyway," she chirps. "And we're only fifty feet from the water."

More like five hundred, but I get the point. I guess in my fantasy world, I'd forgotten that I was actually here on business, to do a job. I'd imagined I was a jet-setting millionaire spiriting away to a vacation spot with his lover. Reality check: Sheila isn't my lover, and only agreed to accompany me on the condition that she not become my lover, and I'm supposed to kill a guy staying at the hotel next door and then get the hell out of Dodge. I guess several months of loneliness and financial deprivation have taken their toll.

But we're here. It's time to get businesslike again. We check in, and I look around. Two double beds. That's good, I don't have to sleep on the floor. We drop the baggage off in the room, which has a strong moldy odor to it, and I tell Sheila she's free to go and sunbathe for a few hours, which was exactly what she had planned. I have some errands to run. She nods, and disappears into the bathroom to change.

I go off to get my sniper rifle.

Gardocki has given me an address, and I ask the hotel clerk where it is, and it turns out it's less than half a mile from the hotel. "Oh, you can walk there," he tells me cheerfully, and I decide it might not be a bad idea. I figure the rifle is going to be discreetly packaged. Perhaps it will even be one of those rifles which comes apart so it can be carried in a custom-made suitcase. I should be able to carry it back without any problems. I set off with my directions to get a ground look at Miami.

I realize I have made a mistake right away. The seediness of my hotel should have been a warning. I hadn't noticed it before, but my beachfront hotel is actually the rule rather than the exception, and the pilot's brand-new luxury tower is probably an attempt by local developers to invigorate the blighted landscape where I have rented a room. I'm in a neighborhood not unlike my own, trashed and neglected, decorated with broken doors and boarded-up windows and trash in the streets. The blazing sun and the race of the inhabitants are the only real differences. Young black men in NFL shirts, which have been picked for their colors rather than from any sense of team loyalty, lounge outside broken-down houses. The first group I see wears shirts from Indianapolis, Tennessee and Kansas City. No one has got a Dolphins shirt on. They eye me suspiciously as I try to put as much distance as I can between myself and them while not crossing the street, an obvious indication of fear.

A boom box is blaring as I get to the end of the first block, and I look to take a right, as my directions suggest, and I see that I'll be walking through a minefield of young black men, many of them hanging out on the sidewalk. I doubt too many white people come down this way. I decide to press on. I'm a hit man. These kids may look tough, but how many of them have actually killed anyone? I look hard into their faces as I walk down the middle of the street and they watch me closely, a white curiosity in the middle of their neighborhood. If black men walked down our streets in Wisconsin, we always noticed, stared. Now I know how it felt for them. Maybe those guys were just looking for an address, too.

"Hey, you," a girl calls from her porch. "Whatcha doin' up this way?" I look over in acknowledgement, not wanting to appear rude or deaf, but not slowing down, either. Something heavy comes flying off one of the porches and bangs into a car which is up on blocks, maybe ten feet behind me. I look at it as it bounces past my feet. Half a baseball. There is some derisive laughter at my obviously startled jump, made embarrassing by my even more obvious attempt to control it.

It is, I realize, a Friday afternoon, a workday. This is my neighborhood in ten years. Not working for these people has become a way of life. Maybe some of them might get night jobs, janitorial work or room service, in the high-end hotels opening up over at the beach, but it's over for them. They'll never own anything or build anything or get off this street. Nobody's even bothering to lie to them anymore that there's a country that cares about them, the lies I believed so completely until the factory closed. These people never had a factory to work in, never felt safe, even for a moment. Their disillusionment is even purer than my own.

I see the second half of the baseball out of the corner of my eye as it comes whizzing just inches from my head. This time I don't startle. There is more derisive laughter. Then one of them, a young boy, yells "Bang." I'll take that over the real thing. They are fantasizing about using me for target practice. To them, I'm Brecht, a symbol of what is wrong with everything. But their anger isn't as fresh as mine, and they let me go. By the time I take a left at the end of the block I sense they've already lost interest in me, just a lost white guy wandering through on his way to somewhere else.

The next three blocks are deserted, except for an old black lady on a porch in a rocking chair who, when I ask her where the inappropriately named Rich Street is, points and says nothing. I find Rich Street, a long alley with no one on it. I hear some voices and follow them, and at the end of the street I see two college-age white kids, in loose T-shirts and backwards baseball caps, polishing surfboards in a garage.

"Hey, man," I say. "I'm looking for 1502 Rich. Am I near it?"

The two look at each other. "Who you looking for?" one asks, returning his eyes to his surfboard.

I look at the piece of paper Gardocki has given me. "Gerald."

"Jerry's inside."

I look around the trashed garage, broken fishing poles and mangled surfboards lying positioned over disused ovens and refrigerators. I don't see a door.

"How do I get in?"

The kid doesn't look up, but stops polishing for a second to mumble, "You gotta push the oven out of the way." I go over and slide the oven to reveal not a door, but a hole in the wall which looks like it was kicked out during a drug frenzy, and the owners just made the best of it and used it as an entrance. I crouch down and manage to wriggle inside, covering myself with drywall dust.

I'm in the kitchen. Two kids are sitting at a table, eating cereal. Between the still-open cereal boxes I see a bong in the middle of the table, and the rich, musky smell of pot is in the air. Dishes are piled in the sink and a roll of paper towels lies partially unrolled across the stained and faded linoleum counter, the only cleaning apparatus in sight. They look alarmed when they both suddenly realize I'm not one of the kids from the garage.

"What's up, man?" one of them says cautiously.

"I'm looking for Jerry."

"JERRY!" screams the kid without moving from his seat, cereal spilling from his mouth back into the bowl with the force of his yell.

"WHAT?" screams back a voice from the living room.

I advance quickly into the living room to prevent any more yelling. Jerry is sitting on a worn gray couch, which used to be white, with his feet propped on a milk crate, watching a muted TV. Copies of *Details, Maxim* and *GQ* in various states of decay litter the floor. One of the magazines, hardened by time and fluids, is being used as a tray for another bong. Jerry turns to look at me. He stiffens when he realizes he doesn't recognize me.

"Hey, dude," he says, sitting straight up, his voice full of caution. "Do I know you?" I detect a slight Wisconsin accent.

"Ken Gardocki sent me," I say. "From Wisconsin."

"Ken who?"

"Gardocki. He gave me your name. Said I could buy . . ." I find myself suddenly unable to describe a rifle. A gun? A weapon? I feel some discretion should be used here. The kid seems skittish enough without me talking openly about firearms.

"Gardocki . . ." the kid says. He's thinking. Slowly. "Is that dude a friend of my dad's?"

"I don't know. Who's your dad?"

"Jerry Grzanka. He used to drive a truck in Wisconsin."

By some miracle, I know the name and the man. I remember him because he had a huge, black handlebar mustache which gave him the appearance of always being in a rage. He was always telling foul, unfunny jokes which usually involved fecal matter. He left the plant about ten years ago, I remember now, to move south because he inherited a house in Florida. Things come together and I look around, hoping for his sake this wasn't the house.

"I know Jerry," I say. "I used to work with him at the plant. Big guy, handlebar mustache."

"Dude!" exults Jerry Junior. "HEY," he screams into the kitchen. "THIS GUY KNOWS MY DAD!" There is no response. Jerry looks at me and shrugs. "So, dude, how much do you need?"

"How much what?"

Jerry looks at me quizzically, becoming suspicious again. He shows me both his palms and shrugs, a gesture which means nothing to me. Then it occurs to me that he thinks I'm here to buy drugs.

"No, man," I tell him. "I'm here for the rifle. Gardocki gave me this address to pick up a rifle." I hand him the slip of paper, which he looks at like a bouncer checking an ID, though all he's looking at is a cocktail napkin with his own address on it. While he is thoroughly examining it, it occurs to me that the chances of me getting a silver metallic suitcase with a scope and sniper rifle unscrewed and fitted nicely into small compartments, as I have imagined, are getting slimmer by the minute.

"Rifle?" Jerry asks.

"He told me this is the place. You're from Wisconsin, right?"

"I lived there when I was eleven," Jerry says, shaking his head.

"Gardocki said he paid you for the rifle already."

Jerry stares at me, mystified. "HEY," he yells into the kitchen. "DID YOU GUYS GET A MESSAGE ABOUT A RIFLE?"

There is silence from the kitchen. Then one of the kids comes in to the living room and says, "There was a message on the machine about it." He picks a pack of cigarettes off the floor, takes one out, lights it and tosses the pack back down amid stained, overturned magazines and ripped carpeting. "I told you about it, man. You were high."

"I wasn't high," says Jerry. "I would've remembered that."

"I told you about it," says the kid, and walks off.

Jerry looks at me and apologizes. "Maybe it was something to do with my dad," Jerry shrugs and gets off the couch. "We have the same name. But he's out of town right now, and he lives across town. Anyway, follow me. I think we've got a rifle in the storage room."

I follow him into the "storage room," which is a former bedroom in which everyone apparently throws their extra crap. There are fishing poles, musical instruments, garbage cans and paintbrushes, but no rifles.

"YOU GUYS SEEN A RIFLE IN HERE?" Jerry screams.

There is some shuffling in the kitchen, then one guy yells, "It's in the bathroom."

Jerry pushes past me and goes into the bathroom, where there is a rifle propped against the toilet. A very old rifle. Jerry picks it up and water from the floor, or at least what I hope is water, drips off the butt.

He hands it to me. "Here you go, dude."

I take the rifle gingerly. It isn't water.

So I offhandedly mention to Jerry that I walked here, and now I have to walk back, carrying a piss-soaked rifle, through a neighborhood where last time they threw heavy objects at me. Jerry tries to adopt the view that the rifle should be good protection, a notion which I reject. But it does bring up the subject of bullets, which I suddenly realize I don't have. After a brief search, six bullets are located in the obvious place, under the kitchen sink.

"I'll give you a ride home," Jerry finally offers, realizing I'm not leaving until this is suggested. As we are leaving, Jerry asks me to follow him back into the bathroom. He digs around behind the toilet for a few seconds, then comes up with . . . a bayonet.

"This goes with it," he tells me.

"Thanks, man. I don't think I'll be needing that."

"But they go together." For some reason, Jerry, who to date hasn't done a thorough job of maintaining this firearm, seems mortified by the possibility that a piece of it might be lost. I take the bayonet, which also has quite recently been pissed on, and we go outside and get into Jerry's car. I place the rifle and bayonet in the back seat, on a pile of enough fast food containers to conceal a body.

We drive back through the hotel parking lot where the clerk, who gave me directions some time back, is standing, staring. Just staring into the parking lot.

"Christ," I say. "Look, man, I can't take the rifle into the room with him just standing there. Can you wait here for a second while I get a blanket?"

"Sure. But I gotta use the john."

"All right. Come in."

We go into the hotel room, and I am hit once again with the stale smell of mold. After the brightness of the outdoors, the motel room, with its drawn blinds and hardly adequate sixty-watt bulb under a dust-blackened shade, is almost like a coal mine. As I strip a blanket off the bed, Jerry thunders back toward the bathroom and nearly crashes into Sheila, who is coming out, in a bikini.

She screams.

He screams.

"Sheila," I say soothingly. "It's all right. He's a friend of mine. I thought you were at the beach."

She looks at me, still shocked, and I can't help but notice how wonderful her body looks, better than I could have imagined. I notice Jerry is looking at her, too, and I begin to feel protective. "Bathroom's free," I tell him. He goes in and closes the door.

Sheila is still looking at me. I think she wants to ask questions, but she also doesn't want to know. She's probably wondering why I'm peering through the blinds, holding the bedspread in my hands, having just allowed a total stranger free run of our hotel room.

"I need you to do me a favor," I tell her.

She reaches for a shawl as she slips into her sandals. "What?"

"That damned clerk is standing in the parking lot. I need you to distract him."

"Distract him from what?"

"Me."

She seems amused by this. "What do you want me to do? A belly dance?" She pulls her shawl on and goes outside as Jerry comes out of the bathroom. As she leaves, Jerry gives me the thumbs-up, an approval of "my woman." I smile at him while I wonder if he's pissed all over the floor.

Sheila goes over to the clerk and says something to him, and they both go into the office together. I run out to the car and get the rifle and bayonet and drag them quickly inside. Jerry and I say our goodbyes as Sheila returns with brochures for the art deco district and South Beach. There's one for a topless beach, which she picks out and hands to me.

I look at it. I wonder what it means if a woman you're interested in starts giving you ads for a topless beach.

"You wanna go?" I ask.

She laughs.

"Thanks," I say, meaning for distracting the clerk, not for the topless beach brochure. She says nothing. But I have a sense of satisfaction. I've handled Step One. The rifle sucks, my car sucks, my hotel room sucks, but there is at least a possibility I can carry out my assignment.

I realize as I lean back on the bed, that this job is every bit as much stress as working on the loading dock during the busy season. I suddenly miss that stress, the comfort of knowing that what you are doing is legal. I wish I still had that job. I wish I still had Kelly. I wish I was back in Wisconsin, coming home from a day full of work, with Kelly already there, making dinner, the evening news on and a light snow falling outside. But it's gone. It's February and it's ninety degrees out and I'm in a Miami hotel room with a stranger, from whom I am concealing a bayonet and a rifle under my bed.

No use crying over the past. Roll with the changes.

Sheila comes back from the beach later that evening while I am watching TV, the blinds drawn. She's got a nice tan coming along. "You want to go to dinner?" I ask her.

"Sure." She slips into the bathroom and showers off the sand while I watch some syndicated 80s family sitcom. I can never remember the names of these shows. There's always a father, a mother, two or three precocious kids and a nice house with furniture I couldn't afford even after the spring season got under way. Not with a car payment. If problems do occur in these shows, they are instantly solved with a long, sincere discussion. The kids always listen and the adults are always worth listening to. No one ever worries about money. No one ever gets laid off. No one ever smokes, for that matter, and it never snows, except in the Christmas episodes. Whose lives are these?

Sheila comes out, a towel wrapped around her and her hair neatly turbaned. She starts doing girl stuff in front of the mirror, where she has arranged eight or nine bottles of various beauty products. "Where do you want to go?" she asks.

"How about some place on the water? You like seafood?"

"Sure."

I continue watching the show. A handsome young father who never seems to work, but nonetheless lives with his girls in a roomy house with antique furniture and hardwood floors, is lecturing his attentive daughter about the evils of drugs. The daughter hasn't actually *used* drugs, but lately she's been hanging around with a girl who might. The scene ends with the daughter nodding, saved from possible drug addiction forever.

This is how they cover it up, I realize. They make shows like this for a reason. They feed us an American dream, how things could be if only we'd close our eyes and just pretend. People watch these shows and feel that they haven't measured up. I'm starting to think that the whole thing is a giant conspiracy, that these shows are funded by the corporations that own the networks, who are in cahoots with the corporations that own tractor-part factories, when Sheila sticks her head around the corner and looks at me.

"Hadn't you better call for reservations?" she asks. "It's Friday night."

She looks stunning. She has put on a short gold dress which shows off every curve, and she is brushing her thick black hair. I like to watch the whole beautification process, the hair brushing, the make-up application. There's something intimate about it. My attention doesn't faze her.

"You look nice," I say.

"Call the restaurant."

Since our arrival in Miami, Sheila has been distant at best, prickly at worst. But after three drinks while we are waiting for a table at the finest seafood restaurant in Miami, a warm glow seems to come over her. I notice she is starting to smile more and become conversational. Maybe it's the view of the ocean, the gulls, the boats passing by. Maybe it's my calm demeanor. Maybe it's the three Big Gulps of Bacardi 151 on what must have been an empty stomach.

"The drinks here are big," she muses, smiling not exactly at me, but at life in general. "Don't you think?"

"They sure are."

"You're nice," she says softly, in her low, raspy voice, and she doesn't sound drunk now.

My first impulse is to ask why, to demand an explanation for a compliment which I feel is largely an error of judgment. Then I remember something I was taught in kindergarten: If people give you a compliment, just thank them and move on. Adult experience has taught me not to get too wrapped up in them because the insults aren't far behind.

"Thanks," I say. It's my first actual compliment from a woman in quite some time. "You're nice too."

She laughs knowingly. I've no idea what she knows. I'm out of the loop. As usual, I can't think of anything to say, and she sits there, smiling at me. Maybe saying nothing is setting the right mood. I smile back, until I start to feel like an idiot, and then, with wondrous timing, our table is called.

I'm wondering what kind of conversation to start as I look at the wine list. I don't want to pry too much into her personal life, but I also don't want to spend the evening talking about the weather. I don't get out enough to waste an evening discussing tides and rain possibilities. I could start telling her about Kelly on the theory that women at any given time like talking about relationships, but I don't actually feel like it. Besides, Sheila doesn't seem the type to fall for the whimpering boyfriend routine.

Sheila looks out the window at the darkening sea and sighs. "My life sucks," she says.

That's a good conversation starter. "Why?"

She tells me about her boyfriend, with whom she has been living for five years. They don't have conversations anymore. He is usually on the road somewhere, and when he's home, he goes out drinking by himself. Or without her, anyway. She tells me about her job, which is shuffling papers for the police department's public relations office. When she had heard rumors the factory was going to close, her uncle, a retired cop, had asked if she'd wanted to join the police department. She'd imagined arresting bad guys and helping people out of burning buildings, and she blushes as she describes her hopes of being able to provide some help for mankind. Then she laughs as she recounts the reality, a job in a musty office in the darkest recesses of the police building. She works for the police public-relations statistician whose job it is to figure out ways of keeping the crime statistics down. So, she explains, if "rape and kidnapping" is made a separate category from "rape," then you can claim that fewer rapes have occurred, and the police department is seen as doing its job.

"So we don't solve or prevent crimes," she says. "We re-name them." News of police impotence in crime solving is comforting to a man who commits them. I wonder if some time down the road she'll be asked to come up with creative ways of describing a series of seemingly random, and hopefully unsolved, murders. Maybe Corinne Gardocki's murder has already been through her hands. Perhaps it was described as "home invasion death by firearm" to keep homicide statistics down.

"So where's the adventure?" she asks me. "Where's the fun? Everything just became so dry all of a sudden." She finishes her drink and looks at me. "That's why I came down here. It was something different. And you've been nice."

I haven't been that nice. I've been preoccupied with buying a pissed-on rifle, and after that, I've been mostly thoughtful and quiet. But if she sees that as nice, who am I to argue?

"So what about you?" she asks.

The inevitable question. What do I say now? This is a hit-man situation I've never thought about. I've rehearsed a thousand times what to say to the cops, but what do I say to someone I don't want to disappoint with a string of lies? I'd like to get closer to her by being honest, not verbally joust with her as if she is an interrogator. I can talk honestly about Kelly, so I figure I'll start there.

"My girlfriend left me," I say. "After the layoffs."

"I know that. That's not what I'm talking about," she says. She doesn't go for it for a second. Women have some kind of sixth sense for sniffing out the information you are trying to conceal. They immediately start digging in the right place, like a bloodhound after a buried bone. "I mean what are you doing here? For Gardocki?"

I must look speechless, because she laughs. "Come on, how bad can it be?"

I laugh too, knowing it is hopeless, but I still try to deflect the question. "How do you know my girlfriend left me?"

"Tony told me."

"What else did he tell you?"

"That you're a good guy. That you've been depressed lately. You need a good woman to cheer you up."

"Is that what he said?"

She shrugs. "Word for word."

I lean across the table flirtatiously. "Are you going to cheer me up?"

She stirs her drink with her finger. I've done it. The conversation is back on safer ground. "Maybe,"she says. Then she leans back in her chair as the waitress arrives with the wine. Right in front of the waitress she asks, "So, what are you doing for Ken Gardocki?"

"I'm just setting up some meetings," I say, after the wine has been poured. I've tasted it as if I can tell one wine from another, and grandly pronounced it acceptable. I've been working on my answer all during the waitress' spiel on the specials, my mind whirring to come up with an answer which would be neither a lie nor an admission of guilt. The final product would impress a philandering congressman, but I was paying no attention to what I ordered.

"That was one of your meetings? That guy today?"

"Yeah."

"He didn't seem like . . ." She trails off.

"Like what?"

"Like the type of person I'd expect you to be hanging around with." She says *you* as if I'm some special, interesting person, a man with his life together and his goals and dreams clearly outlined.

"Thank you," I say. No offense to Jerry, but I'm flattered that people find us an odd couple.

Sheila shrugs. "You don't have to tell me if you don't want to," she says, making it clear that further reticence on my part will disappoint her completely, and destroy any chances I have of not sleeping alone tonight, but she's willing to accept it.

"I'll tell you one day," I say. Maybe. "I want to buy a convenience store back home. I want to run it. I need the money from Gardocki to buy the store, so I'm just doing him a couple of favors."

This intrigues her. We talk about the store. We talk about things we want to do with our lives. Sheila wants to quit the police department and have three kids and sell homemade goods over the Internet. She has quite a flair for crafts. I want to run a convenience store, and three kids sounds like a nice number. We're feeling each other out for something long term here, and just when I think the whole Gardocki line of questioning has been forgotten, she says, "You don't seem like someone who'd work for Gardocki."

"He's not so bad."

"But he hires . . . criminals. I've met the people who 'do him favors.' They're criminals, Jake. You don't seem like that."

I'm a late bloomer, I almost say. Fortunately, my internal spin doctor comes up with a better response. "It won't be much longer."

She looks at me, clearly worried. "These meetings . . . are they dangerous?"

I think about the answer, perhaps too long.

"Let's talks about something else," Sheila says. She starts mentioning that while she was at the beach today, she saw a man parasailing, and she would like to give it a try tomorrow, if time permits. While she is talking, I say, "Yes, they're dangerous."

She stops talking. "Do you think you'll be okay?"

Her concern is touching. I've been alone so long, taken the hardest hit of my life with no support, that I never imagined anyone would care about me again. All those days walking back and forth to the library, I figured it was over for me. Love, romance, work: Those were things of the past. The misery was so real, I didn't think that things might turn around for me. It creates a fear. For the first time since I took on this hit-man career, I find myself afraid of being caught. I have something to lose. I look into her brown eyes, see her thick, dark hair falling on her shoulders, notice the smooth skin on her neck. I don't want those to be memories I have while I'm waiting on death row in a Florida prison.

"I think I'll be fine," I say shakily. I nod my head once or twice to reassure her, but I can tell she is not convinced. "We'll go para-sailing in the afternoon."

She smiles at me, but it's a sad smile, as if she's never going to see me again.

It's five thirty in the morning and I can hear traffic. People are going to work. I lie in bed and look at the stained, moldy ceiling and won-der about their lives, these people who go to work so early in Miami. I've never met any of them, I'm sure, but any one could change my life, simply by calling a cop on a cell phone when they see me outside a Miami motel with a very big rifle.

I can feel Sheila's heartbeat as she sleeps next to me, hear her gentle breathing. I stroke her arm, partly out of affection, partly to determine if she's deep enough asleep that I can carefully wriggle away from her and get out of bed. She doesn't stir. My other arm is under her side, and I gently pull it out.

"Mmmmph," she says, and rolls over and sighs, her eyes still closed. She mumbles something and I think she is talking to me, then realize she is dreaming. I sit next to her on the bed for a few seconds, watching her sleep, stroking her hair. She is a beautiful woman. I want to spend the day watching her sleep, enjoying the peace of this moment, remembering the night before. I think of the moment when we returned from a walk on the beach, and I took my shoes off to get into my bed, expecting her to get into hers, and the thrill I felt when she cuddled up next to me and with a tipsy smile asked, "What're we going to do now, Jake?" I liked hearing her say my name.

I pull my jeans on quietly, then my socks and shoes. I can hear someone snoring in the next room, the same guy who was banging on the wall a few hours earlier, tired of the moaning and squeaking bedsprings he must have been listening to for hours before he finally lost his temper. We were louder than either of us realized. After that, we giggled for a few moments, enjoying the irritation we had caused, then both drifted off to sleep. I had forgotten to set an alarm, but woke up in time anyway, the novelty of having someone beside me again shaking my sleep patterns.

Sheila's gold dress is lying on top of my open suitcase, and I drape it on my bed, careful not to crumple it. I regard it for a second, laid out on the bed. It looks so small. Without her in it, it is just a piece of gold cloth. I take a white T-shirt out of my suitcase and pull it on, then reach under the bed and extract the rifle and the bayonet. I pull the bedspread off the bed and wrap it around the rifle.

I debate for a second whether to take the bayonet. What the hell am I going to do with it, charge him like Sergeant York if I can't make the shot? I think about tossing it back under the bed, but I like the feel of it, the heavy weight. Having it gives me some kind of psychological lift. I slip it into my belt loop, stand up, and see myself in the mirror. My hair is everywhere. I look like I've been having sex all night.

I try slicking my hair back, and it just pops back into the messy bed-head shape it was in earlier. No point worrying about that. Hopefully I won't be meeting too many people. I pat my pocket. Room key, check. My wallet is on the dresser. Check. Don't want that with me. I lean over and give Sheila a kiss on the cheek. She murmurs.

Time to go kill a pilot.

Outside, it is still dark, but there is a subtle hue in the sky that indicates dawn is coming quickly. I go out onto the beach, where I can hear gulls squawking and I notice the roar of the ocean is much softer than it was last night. The ocean has moved. The tide is out.

It's way out. The tide has pulled back at least one hundred yards. I sit down beside the motel's air-conditioning unit and look out at the sea, realizing that there is no way I can hit anything in the water from here. Maybe if I had a brand-new rifle with a scope and a tripod, and a silencer, it would be possible. But with this piss-soaked relic from World War II, I can't make this shot. The guy from *Saving Private Ryan* couldn't make this shot. I lean back against the air conditioner, listening to the steady hum of its motor, thinking of an excuse to tell Ken Gardocki.

Just for practice, I hold the rifle up and look along the barrel at the sea, pointing it at a black pier far off in the distance. I get a whiff of piss. No matter how many times I wipe the stock, the urine smell seems to be permanently ingrained into the wood. I toss the rifle down. It's not possible. Gardocki will just have to deal with it. Of course, if I come back without killing this guy, there's not going to be any convenience store for me and Tommy, and Gardocki is going to start screaming about getting the money back that he's laid out sending me and Sheila to Miami. I'll be back where I started, owing a gangster money and not having any coming in. I think of things to tell him. Maybe I can tell him the pilot never showed up. Maybe he'll believe that the pilot never went swimming at six in the morning, he changed his plans. He'll just have to deal with it. But then what? Am I supposed to go home and sit in my icebox of an apartment and try and talk Sheila into leaving her boyfriend so she can move in with an unemployed hit man who lies to his clients about not being able to find his targets?

Then I see a figure wearing bathing shorts heading to the water.

Fuck it. I'm here. It's worth a try. I lie down in the sand and watch the tiny figure testing the water, going into the waves. I'm getting the adrenaline rush now, and I know it is going to happen. I pick the piss-soaked rifle up and inch forward, and try to draw a bead on him.

There's no way. He's a mile away and he's moving around. It's getting light out, too. Five minutes ago I was here in almost darkness, and now I can see down the beach. In minutes, it will be full day-light, and people might wonder why I'm crawling around in the sand with a rifle. I hop up and dart fifty yards closer, fifty yards across an open beach with no cover, and I lie down again. From here, I look over and I can see the pilot's ten-story hotel. Only one or two rooms have lights on.

He is swimming. I can see the occasional limb come up and splash down again, but the shot is still too far. The beach is still clear. I hop up again and close the distance by another fifty yards.

That's it. I fling myself down in the sand and draw a bead again. He stops swimming momentarily, stands to catch his breath, and I fire.

BANG.

I think the rifle has exploded in my hands and taken half my head with it. I wasn't holding it tightly enough and the weapon has bucked and bashed against my head, so the ringing in my ears this time is partly from the noise and partly from the impact of the butt against my skull. I stick my head up to see.

I don't see him.

God, did I get him? He's gone! I'm about to leap up and run back to the hotel, but I decide to wait a few more seconds for some form of confirmation, maybe a glimpse of a lifeless torso rolling lazily in with the waves. Maybe from this distance I could even see streaks of blood in the water. Then I see him spring up from the breakers and shake water out of his hair.

The sonofabitch was underwater. And I missed him completely. He didn't even hear the shot. He comes walking in from the sea and I fire again.

BANG.

This time I'm gripping the rifle much tighter, but it still tries to jerk away from me. How could anyone ever hit anything with this piece of shit? The pilot hears that one. I see him stop and look around.

"Fuck!" I scream to myself. BANG BANG BANG BANG click. That's it. Maybe I'm out of ammo, maybe there's sand in this piece of shit. Either way, it's done firing. I can still see the bastard. I haven't even nicked him. The pilot is in the water, crouching, trying to figure out what all that shooting is about. He sees me.

He starts running toward his hotel.

Oh shit. I hop up, still carrying the useless rifle. It's a foot race now. He's slowed down by the surf, I'm slowed down by the sand. It's too far, I'm not going to get him. I run in toward the sea, where the sand has been smoothed out by the tide, and I get more speed. Holy God, he's going to get away. Fuck fuck fuck . . .

He trips on something.

He goes down, splashing wildly as he tries to right himself, then falls again. I close the distance quickly. He gets up, sees me coming at him full tilt, then turns and bounds back further into the sea.

He's going to try to swim away from me. Where's he going to go, England? I'm close enough now to hear him yelling to himself as he thrashes, jumping up into each breaker. If he gets into deep water, he could hide, I realize. I splash out after him, still holding the rifle, the water waist-deep now. My shoes and socks are like concrete.

A wave comes in and nearly knocks me down. When I look around, he is gone.

Damn.

I stumble out a few more feet, drop the rifle into the water and reach into my back pocket for the bayonet. The thing is really nothing more than a sharpened spike with a very heavy metal end where it is supposed to attach to the rifle. It would be a good club, because the spike has no blade, so you can actually hold it and hit with the weighted end. I look around as the tide goes out. Nothing. He's staying underwater.

Two can play that game. Another wave comes in and I drop to my knees and go under, the salty water filling my mouth and burning my eyes. Still holding the bayonet, I wriggle toward the spot where I last saw him. Nothing.

Frantically, I look toward the beach, expecting to see him
streaking across the sand to the hotel. Nothing. That's good, at least,
he's still in the water. It is daylight now. Way down the beach I can
see a figure jogging towards us, with two dogs. I low-crawl along
in the surf, alligator-like, keeping nothing but my head above the
water and my hands walking along pebbly ground. I'm cutting my
hands to bits as I walk on them, my knuckles dragging across
seashells and debris.

The tide is going out, dragging me away from the shoreline,
exposing me. It exposes him too. I see the bastard.

He raises his head slightly out of the water, not even five feet
away, and I hear him gasping for air, trying to keep his desperate
breaths quiet. He is facing the hotel, and he turns and looks frantically around. He doesn't see me because he's looking for someone standing straight up, not bothering to check the surf around
him. He tries to push through the surf towards the beach, convinced
he's lost me. I think not. In my alligator crawl, I'm much quicker.
The tide, crashing into the beach, carries me right into him. I'm on
him in a second.

His head starts to turn. The heavy end of the bayonet thunks
down on his head. He still moves toward the hotel, but more
slowly now. His legs are giving out. I bring back my arm and thunk
him again, this time with all the strength I have. I hear the skull
cracking. His legs buckle and he goes down into the waves.

Grabbing his limp arm, I start pulling him back into the surf. I'm
gripping his arm tightly as I pull him through one set of breakers
after another. The jogger with the two dogs is coming up on me,
a hundred yards and closing. I keep pulling the pilot out into the
waves, farther, farther. I push his body down and stand on him
while I take off my shirt. The jogger runs past, and I wave. He
doesn't wave back. Guess he didn't see me after all.

I pull the pilot out another ten or fifteen yards, and it suddenly
occurs to me that I'm swimming with a bleeding body in waters
where there have been recent shark attacks. I let him go, give him

a push toward England, hoping a giant shark will come out of nowhere and devour the evidence, or a strong tide will whisk him off to Liverpool.

The body pops right to the surface and bobs around. I drop the bayonet and start swimming back in.

When I reach the water's edge, I walk out slowly.

I grab the bedspread I have left by the air conditioner, shake it out, put it back on the bed the second I return to the hotel room. Then I hop in the shower. I scrub every piece of sand and sea residue off me, condition my hair. Then I get back into bed with Sheila and pull the covers over myself. She stirs.

"Where'd you go?" she mumbles sleepily.

"I just took a shower."

"Mmmmph." She rolls over and puts her hand on my chest.

I look at my watch. Six forty-five. The whole thing has taken less than an hour.

"I thought I heard the door open," Sheila says.

"Nah."

Her eyes open and I can see her looking at me, and I prepare for her to start calling me a liar, demanding explanations. She is going to say something, something final, something devastating. She is awake now. "You still want to go parasailing today?" she asks.

"Sure."

She smiles. Her eyes close again, and in a few minutes, she is breathing steady and solid, the relaxed breaths of someone lost in a pleasant dream.

NINE

I'm back at the convenience store. I have to work the next seven days, because Tommy has been working non stop as a result of my traveling, and needs some time off. I'm rearranging a potato chip display, putting all the Wenke products on the bottom shelf. I'd put them in the storage shed if there was room. I see Ken Gardocki pull up, fill his SUV with gas. He's driving his own car. Times are tough for everyone. I guess with Karl out of the picture, there's a job opening around here for a chauffeur.

Gardocki isn't smiling when he comes into the Gas'n'Go. He makes himself a soda, then comes to the counter, pulls a pack of cigarettes from the counter display and asks, "So, what happened, Jake?"

I'm surprised by his expression. "Everything went well," I say softly, cheerfully. Loudly, I add, "That's three fifty for the smokes,

ninety-nine cents for the soda, and twenty-six dollars for the gas."
I ring it up and give him the total.

He gives me the money. "Jerry Grzanka called me. He said you
never picked up the rifle."

I squint at him. "What the hell's he talking about? I picked it up."

Gardocki sips his soda, looking at me across the top of his
straw, a hard, studying look. "Why," he asks, "do you suppose, that
Gerald Grzanka, a man I have known all my life, would tell me that
you didn't?"

"You've known that guy all your life?" Despite my certainty that
no one will ever come down to look at our security tapes again, I
keep glancing at them nervously. There's something intimidating
about being videotaped, about the knowledge that your every
action is being recorded for posterity. It forces you to be honest,
but it also forces you into a mentality of submission. Maybe that's
why Gas'n'Go likes it, so it can turn all the men and women who
work there into so many lab rats. "Let's go outside," I say.

"Why?" Gardocki doesn't budge. He turns and faces a video camera and yells at it, "WHY THE FUCK DO YOU SUPPOSE MY LIFE-
LONG FRIEND GERALD GRZANKA LIED TO ME?" Then he stares
into the camera, as if waiting for an answer.

Okay, this is odd. Now I'm going to have to erase this tape.
What's even odder is that Gardocki is asking a legitimate question.

Ken is staring at me. "Ken," I say very softly, in an attempt to
lower the decibel level of the conversation. "I don't know what's
going on. Why don't we go outside?"

"SO YOU'RE TELLING ME THAT YOU KILLED THE PILOT,"
Gardocki yells at the camera.

"WILL YOU SHUT THE FUCK UP!" I explode, as a mother and
young daughter walk into the store, stare at us, then walk out.
"Great, that's a customer you just cost me." I'm already acting like
the store is mine. "Look, I don't know what this dipshit is telling
you, but—"

"He is not a dipshit, sonny," Gardocki hisses. "I trust that man with my life. And if he tells me you didn't pick up the rifle, you didn't pick up the rifle."

"I picked up the rifle," I tell him.

Gardocki backs away from the counter, holding his cigarettes and his soda, shaking his head in disgust. "We were in Vietnam together," he says. "You're going to tell me that a guy I went to Vietnam with—"

"That kid wasn't even twenty years old," I say.

Gardocki stops. He stares at me. "What?"

"Jerry Grzanka. That little pot-smoking freak. He wasn't even twenty years old. He gave me a goddamned rifle that he'd been using to prop his toilet tank lid open. It was a piss-soaked piece of crap from World War II and I couldn't hit a damned thing with it," I rant. "What the hell kind of crackpot idea did you come up with, anyway? Who do you think I am, Lee Harvey Fucking Oswald? You nearly got me killed, you sonofabitch. Do you have any idea how close that guy came to getting away? I had to chase him—"

"Twenty years old?" asks Gardocki.

I am breathless. "Something like that. I didn't ask."

"Was he a heavy kid? With, you know, sandy hair?"

"Yeah."

"That's Jerry's son."

"Yeah," I say. "I worked with his dad for a year or two, on the loading docks. I remember him. Big guy, funny mustache."

Gardocki is thinking hard now. "So you got a rifle from Grzanka's son."

"Yeah."

"Why didn't you get the rifle from the old man?"

"Jesus, Ken, I went to the address you gave me and asked for a guy named Gerald. That's what you told me to do."

"I meant Gerald, not Jerry. Jerry Junior's an idiot."

"No shit."

Gardocki starts laughing. He steps up to the counter again. "Shit, Jake, I must have given you his old address. It's some beat-up house he lets his son live in." Gardocki shakes his head at his own forgetfulness. "He moved a few years ago."

I nod. I'm still a little upset about how quickly Gardocki turned on me.

"Jake, Grzanka had a nice rifle for you. A real beaut. It cost me two grand. Had a scope and everything."

"A silencer?"

"I don't know about a silencer," he says, "but it came apart, and fit into a briefcase, like you wanted. Isn't that what you wanted?"

I nod. "It would have been nice."

"So how'd you kill this guy, then?" Gardocki is still laughing.

"I had to chase him up and down the beach with a bayonet."

Gardocki is guffawing now. "A bayonet," he roars, and I glance nervously toward the video camera. I'm going to have to *burn* this tape, but Gardocki's laughter is almost contagious, and I find myself chuckling as I recount blazing away at the pilot with my piss-soaked, sand-clogged rifle, to no avail, then splashing around after him in the waves, pretending to be an alligator. The alligator detail brings Gardocki to tears.

He wipes his eyes. "Oh, Jake, you're a crazy sonofabitch," he says. "How about the girl? You get any?"

I nod quickly, not wanting to bring Sheila into it.

"Give her the high hard one, eh?" he laughs, but I don't laugh back, and he picks up on it quickly. "Serious, eh?"

"I dunno. We'll see."

"Well, good for you." He nods at me, but I feel he is genuinely happy for me, and I find it almost touching. "Anyway, come by my office tomorrow. Got some money for you, maybe a little more work."

A little more work? How many people does Gardocki need killed? I'd assumed the pilot job might be the end of it. I'm back

on my feet now, I have some cash, I've got the possibility of a woman, I'm not as angry as I was before. I'm losing the fire in the belly that got me to where I am. My problems are disappearing right before my eyes, and if it's all the same to Gardocki, I'd really rather not murder anyone else for a while.

"Sure, Ken," I say cautiously. "Talk to you tomorrow."

He laughs as he walks out. "Ya crazy bastard," he says as the door closes behind him.

I go back into the security room and take the tape out, pop in another one. I am about to throw the tape in the dumpster when I have my latest paranoid thought . . . what if someone went through the dumpster and found it? That alone could get me convicted. I break the plastic and pull out the videotape, then get a steel bucket from the back. When no one is around, I go out to the gas pumps and squirt a tiny amount of gasoline into the bucket, then, later in the shift, take the mess out behind the dumpster and toss a lit cigarette in the bucket. WHOOSH. One less problem.

I suddenly realize there is a security camera out by the pumps, so now there is a tape of me burning the tape.

This is a lot like being a loading dock manager. There's the tireless checking and re-checking, the necessary attention to detail. The factory trained me for this. As I drop the second tape in the bucket, leaving the VCR temporarily empty, I think to myself that all I did was put the skills to a different use. That's what they get for taking my job away.

I get home that night and there are three messages from Sheila. She's been thinking about me. I can't call her back because her trucker boyfriend is home, so I just listen to the messages over and over again, enjoying the sound of her voice. Between her messages there's another message, from Tommy, asking where the hell I put some keys. I figure he found them or he would have called every ten minutes. So while listening to Sheila's message three or four

times, to figure if I missed anything, I also have to listen to Tommy
bitch at me over and over. Finally I figure I'm just acting like a high
school kid and I erase them all.

I step outside to get something from my car, and when I come
back, I have a new message. Dammit! I was only gone three minutes, and that was probably the last time Sheila is going to call
tonight. I hit the play button on the machine.

I know you killed Corinne Gardocki, says a man's muffled voice.
I know all about it. I want ten grand and I won't go to the cops.

So much for my troubles melting away.

I know you killed Corinne Gardocki says the tape, and Gardocki
keeps hitting Rewind and listening to it. *I know you killed Corinne
Gardocki . . . I know you killed Corinne Gardocki . . . I know you
killed Corinne Gardocki.*

We are standing out in a field, which is where Gardocki likes to
talk business. A different field each time, just in case the cops start
bugging a field. I think he's getting a little carried away with the
security measures, but better safe than sorry.

"Jesus, Ken, will you stop that?" The voice is starting to give me
the willies. Gardocki is nodding wisely as he listens to each replay
of the tape. He ignores me. I *know you killed Corinne Gardocki. I
know you killed . . .*

"Listen to this," he says cheerfully. He pulls a tape from the con-
sole in between the seats of his SUV and takes mine out. *I know
you killed your wife,* says the same voice. Ken replays it over and
over with an evil smile. *I know you killed your wife . . . I know you
killed your wife . . . I know . . . .*

"It's the same person," I say.

"Yeah." He is grinning. "Except it's not the same thing at all."

"Why not?"

"Because you have a listed telephone number. I don't. Only one
person knows my number who also knows you."

I think for a minute. "Jeff Zorda?"

"Bingo." Gardocki laughs. "That was the job I wanted to talk to you about. I was going to play you my tape, then you brought your own, and that kind of cinched the deal. I thought it was Zorda, but I wasn't sure until I heard yours."

"You want me to kill Zorda?" There have been times when I thought I'd like to kill Zorda, but that was back before actually killing people was such a reality. You can't just go and kill people you've worked with, watched football games with, drunk beers with. People who do that aren't right in the head. "Why don't I just go and have a talk with him?"

Gardocki is looking at me, clearly amused. He seems to be in good spirits today. The unveiling of his blackmailer is a real mood enhancer. "You're tired of this, aren't you?"

I see understanding in his eyes. He knows people. It's the quality I always liked about him, back when I hardly knew him and used to place bar bets at his table before the Packers games. "A little bit. Yeah."

"Gettin' laid did it." Gardocki shakes his head. "Remember what I told you, about men with women? You get a single guy, you're on much better ground. It's only a few more rolls in the hay and you're telling her everything."

"I wouldn't do that." But he doesn't believe me. He's giving me the same look he was giving me in the convenience store when he thought I was lying about the pilot. Lately, I've begun wondering how much Gardocki trusts me. Admittedly, it's a stressful situation, us both having to trust each other completely, but that thing with the pilot unnerved me a little. And him screaming at the video cameras was just no way for a self-respecting career criminal to behave. It occurs to me, for a second, that I might be better at this than he is, more suited for it psychologically. "I don't want to do it anymore because I've got it out of my system," I say. "My life isn't destroyed anymore. I'm putting the pieces back together."

Gardocki looks at me, and I think he knows that I was just thinking I could do his job, be the town's head criminal, better than him.

He has that way of looking through you, like he understands everything that makes you tick. He's better than the cops. Maybe, if I ever decided to run the crime in this town, I'd need to learn a look like that. But I don't want to run the crime here. I want to run a convenience store, and have a woman to come home to.

"Pop this bastard," Gardocki says.

"I'll talk to him."

"Pop him. Kill him. Waste him. Dump his fucking body in a lime pit somewhere."

"Lime pit?"

"Then pour gasoline on him and grind up his skull. No dental records. Nothing."

"I'll talk to him."

"Listen to the tape, Jake." He flips on the tape recorder again, and plays me Zorda's greatest hit. *I know you killed your wife. . . . I know you killed your wife.*

"I'll talk to him."

Gardocki tosses the tape recorder back in the SUV and pulls out a brown leather pouch. He hands it to me. "Take a gun just in case the conversation doesn't go so good."

I shrug. It's sound advice.

I'm supposed to go over to Zorda's place and kill him, or talk to him, whichever is most convenient, but what I really want to do is go over to the police building and drop in on Sheila and ask her to lunch. I've hardly seen her since we got back from Miami, and we're always missing each other with the phone calls. Her boyfriend is going out on the road again tonight, so I'll be free to call after about nine o'clock, and perhaps I should swing by the grocery store to get something for dinner for her. I'm not a bad cook. Maybe I should go by the florist and pick up a rose. I bet that fat bastard she lives with hasn't given her a rose in some time, if ever. I'll need for this

Zorda thing to go quickly, whatever the outcome, because the florist will probably close at five and it's almost three now.

As I pull onto Zorda's street, I think about Sheila's boyfriend. I wonder how much trouble he's going to cause when she tries to leave him for me. Of course, there's the obvious solution. I could "run into him" at one of his truck stops and leave him in a dumpster, making the whole problem moot. But that's the Jake that needs to disappear now. I'm trying to work myself away from the habit of shooting people who make my life hard. I have the possibility of rebuilding something, here. What kind of husband, father and small-business owner regularly offs people? No, I'm going to have to talk to him, reason with him. Maybe he, Sheila and I can have a talk someplace. That'll be a miserable evening. I pull up outside Zorda's apartment and unzip the leather pouch, let the weight of the pistol fall into my hand. I look at it, the weight comforting, the chrome plating giving me a sense of glamour and power. Dammit, the truckstop-dumpster idea is just so tempting. Sheila would never have to know.

No, no, no. What kind of way is that to start a relationship?

I tuck the pistol into my belt and go and knock on Zorda's door.

"Hey," says Zorda as he opens the door, and he says it . . . just a bit off. He knows why I'm here and he thinks I'm going to kill him. It's nothing specific I can put my finger on, it's just a feeling that things aren't right between us. There isn't a smoothness, a relaxed be-who-you-are quality to his greeting, nor to mine, but we're both trying hard to pretend the smoothness is there.

"Come on in, Jake." Maybe I *can* put my finger on it. I haven't been over to his apartment since the layoffs, and he doesn't ask why I'm here now. And he's pale. I imagine I can smell fear on him as he offers to take my coat. *Take my coat?* Does he think I'm royalty? Yes, there's definitely something wrong. If he hadn't left a blackmailing message on my answering machine, instead of "Take your coat?" I'd be hearing "What do you want, fuckface?"

I've seen movies where mob guys pay a visit to someone they're going to whack. There's this supposed tension and strained dialogue, as they all know what's going to happen but no one wants to say it. I've always wondered about those scenes. Do they ever really happen? What a waste of energy, beating around the bush like that. I wouldn't work out as a mob hit man. I take the tape out of my pocket and toss it on the chipped veneer of Zorda's coffee table.

"What up with that tape, man?" I ask

Zorda looks at me, not at the tape. "What are you talking about?"

A person who hadn't left the message would be looking at the tape, not into my eyes to try to determine his future. Then he glances down at my belt, trying to determine if I've got a gun or not. It's in the back of my belt, and he can't see it. "Sit down," I say, pointing at the couch.

He remains standing. "What are you talking about?" he asks again. "I've never seen that tape before."

That much is probably true. It's spent its whole life in my answering machine, and I doubt he has actually *seen* the tape. He's trying to stick to the truth here, with the correct wording and the omissions of a liar. It's too easy to spot.

"How'd you figure it out?" I ask.

"How'd I figure what out? Jake, man, what're you talking about?" Now he smiles, a totally inappropriate gesture of submission. Someone has come into his house and accused him of something and he's acting conciliatory, submissive. The real Jeff Zorda would have screamed at me to get the fuck out of his apartment. His jerky, inappropriate smile and fruitless protestations of ignorance are starting to annoy me.

"Sit down," I say angrily. "Are we going to fuck around all afternoon?"

"Jake, man, do you want a beer or something?" he asks, and he's about to run off into the kitchen, so I have no choice but to pull the gun. Gardocki was right. This would have been a disaster without the gun. Zorda freezes. His face lights up with terror, and he starts taking another step backwards and he still might run to the kitchen, so I point the gun right at his nose.

"Just. Sit. Down."

"Jake man, I swear—"

"Please, for the love of God, just sit down."

"I swear I don't know what you're talking about, Jake, what's the matter with you. Let me get you a beer—"

"JEFF!" I scream. I'm holding the gun about a foot from his head, and I speak very steadily. "I'm going to shoot you in the face. Do you understand that? I'm going to shoot you in the face right here in your living room, if you don't sit down."

He stares at me, thankfully silent.

"SIT THE FUCK DOWN!" I'm losing my cool here. Terrified people are not easy to deal with. I can see myself popping a few rounds in him just for being scared. But that's not the way I want to be anymore. I need to think of getting my life back together. I think of Sheila, sitting at her desk, altering crime statistics with a look of boredom. I take a long, deep breath as Zorda finally, mercifully, sits down.

"Jake," he says, his voice quivering. "Jake, I don't know what—"

"SHUT UP!" I'm not ready for this, the begging and denying. Maybe I understand the mob way, now. Maybe the calm conversations which overshadow the real meaning are just a way of giving the hit man an easy time of it. I wish Zorda had seen a few of those movies. "I want you to shut up and listen to me, okay?"

"Jake, whatever you think someone did to you, it wasn't me."

"I'm going to ask you some questions. You're going to answer those questions. If you answer all the questions honestly, completely honestly, you get to live. Do you understand?"

The mention of a possibility of living through this encounter gives Zorda an instant attack of nervous breathing, the hope of life swelling up in him, the fear pouring out. I let him pant for a few seconds as I look around his apartment. It is a lot like mine, except his cable service is stolen and his TV is nicer. I like what he's done with the walls, beige paint giving the place a homier feeling than the off-white I have at my place. He's always been good with plants, too. I should learn that. A few gardening techniques really come in handy when trying to make a house a home. Kelly took all the plants and I've never really thought about replacing them. I look back over at Zorda, who has become a sweaty mess.

"You want a smoke?" I ask.

"Yes," he says. I take out my pack and we both grab a cigarette and light them.

"I like what you've done with your place," I tell him.

He exhales. "Thanks." He is still staring around, wide-eyed, wondering if every second of conversation will be his last, and discussing his furnishings is hardly a priority of his right now.

"Do you understand . . . about being completely honest?"

He nods.

"Okay. Question one. How did you figure it out?"

He exhales again, not looking me in the eye. "You went out of town," he says softly. "I went by the convenience store looking for you, and Tommy said you'd left town."

"So what?"

"He said it real funny."

Tommy, dammit. That guy never could tell a decent lie. Oh, well. That should make him a good business partner.

"Then he started talking about how you guys were going to buy the store," Jeff continues. "Where do you get the money to leave town and buy a store? And I just started thinking."

I'm thinking about having a talk with Tommy, but Zorda's on a roll. Now that I've got him talking, he won't stop.

"I started thinking about that conversation we had in Tulley's, when I told you Ken Gardocki offered me money to kill his wife. And I put two and two together. Shit, Jake, you didn't even have money for smokes two months ago. I know they don't pay that much at the freakin' Gas'n'Go."

I am about to ask another question, about how the whole black-mail payment was to have been arranged, when Zorda starts up again.

"Fuck, Jake, it wasn't fair, man," he tells me. "It wasn't fair. He asked me if I wanted to do it, then when I asked about it a few days later, he said he'd changed his mind. Acted like he had just been joking. I needed the money, man. I can't live like this, waiting for the fucking mailman to bring me my fucking unemployment check." His voice cracks and he starts crying. "I just need to have something to fucking *do*, man, you know what I mean? I don't even care what it is anymore. I just need to *do* something. Do you know? Can you understand that?" He looks at me imploringly.

"Of course."

"And you got the fucking job," he says. "He gave you my fucking job. That asshole."

"Jeff, man, I'm sorry."

"Fuck you! I could have done it. I would have done a great job. Why couldn't he see that? What's the matter with me, man? Why do people always pick you over me?"

"What are you talking about?"

"I'm talking about that, man. I'm talking about the factory. You remember that? You remember that?"

"Remember what?" The hand with the gun in it has gone flaccid, the pistol resting against my thigh. I look at Zorda, tears streaming down his face, and I wonder if he's losing his mind, if fear is making him babble incoherently. But he isn't that scared any more. "What, Jeff? What are you talking about?"

"That should have been my job, at the factory. They should have promoted *me* to loading dock manager. But they didn't. Why? Why is it always you? Why don't you just go ahead and kill me, you fuck. Just get it over with. You've ruined my life anyway."

I can barely remember what he's talking about. Eight years ago, they told the forklift guys there was a promotion available on the loading docks. I filled out the forms, got an interview, and got the job. Jeff, Tommy and I went out and celebrated. It never occurred to me that Jeff might have applied too, and I knew Tommy was looking for something administrative. He eventually got it. But after eight years, Zorda was still working the forklifts.

"What was it, man, my SAT scores? Did you do real good on the SATs, or something? I mean, what? Why does everyone go to you over me?" He is sobbing now, and I start to say something, but he starts again. "Shit, you remember that game," he sobs and sniffles. "That football game? You picked five plays in a row. I mean, how the hell can anyone pick five plays in a row? We had a bet, remember? You took me for fifty bucks. Five plays in a row! You're the luckiest sonofabitch alive, and you always win, Jake. You always fucking win."

I always win? That's a new way of looking at my life. "Jeff, there was a TV behind you showing the game a few seconds ahead. Didn't you ever figure that out?"

He stops sobbing and wipes his eyes, then wipes his nose on his sleeve. "What?"

"When I won the football bet. There was a TV behind you that was picking up a signal. I was just watching the TV, man. I was going to tell you about it but you went and got coked up without saying goodbye to anyone." I laugh, and look into his tortured eyes. I guess no matter how bad things got for me, they were always worse for him, because, I realize, Zorda just isn't that smart. It's endearing. I almost want to hug him, this guy who has spent his whole life intimidated by, and jealous of, me. Me, for God's sake.

He watches me laugh, and he thinks I'm laughing at him. I am. But I'm also laughing at the whole fucked-up nature of everything. Look at him, ready to turn me into the cops unless I gave him money. Look at me, sitting in his living room with a pistol, ready to splatter his brains across his own living room. I'm laughing because the world's a mess, and he starts laughing because he realizes I'm not going to kill him.

"I'll take that beer," I tell him.

We spend the next hour chatting like old times. I tell him I'm retiring so that I can run a convenience store. I'm going to hook him up with Gardocki, who seems to have a never-ending supply of people who need killing. Maybe that's the sign of a life not well lived, knowing all these people who have to die. Maybe the ones who need to be killed are the ones with the lives not well lived. Whatever. I describe killing people to him, and he listens with rapt attention, learning the tricks of the trade. I give him a list of do's and don't's. We finish off a six-pack. It's a quarter to five when I look at my watch, and mention I need to buy some roses for Sheila.

Sheila's boyfriend leaves at nine, and she's in my apartment at 9:35. I remember the smell of her perfume the second she walks in, and I give her a kiss hello. It takes me right back to the hotel room in Miami. She tosses her purse on my couch as I take a roast out of the oven and the smell fills the room.

"How was your day?" she asks.

"God, it was a stressful one. Everything worked out okay, though. How about yours?"

She sees the dining-room table set, candles out, gives a squeal of delight when she notices the roses. She comes and puts her arms around me. "It was okay," she whispers in my ear, and smiles. "It's better now."

TEN

It's been a long, hard few months.

Gardocki got us the loan and we bought the store. We're still working for Gas'n'Go, which is affiliated with Amalgamated Something-or-Other, which is a division of some other corporation, but basically, it's our store. They tell us to put Wenke products on the top shelf, but it's really up to us if we want to do it or not. I don't. Fuck Wenke. Tommy doesn't understand why I feel this way, says they're good potato chips and we should try to sell them. Sometimes, after I take over the store, I see he's put them all on the top shelf. Sometimes, I throw them down onto floor level. I figure I'll stop doing that one day.

It's going to be a while until we start making money. The loans are killing us for the time being. I start to sweat sometimes when we don't get a rush in the morning, and coffee goes unsold. I tally it up in my head, the cost of the coffee we throw out. The gas sales

are pretty steady, though, and Tommy tells me not to sweat. We figure in about two years, we'll be making about twenty-five grand
each, and we're working about sixty hours a week. It's easy,
though, and it's a whole different deal when you're doing it for
yourself.

Jughead got a raise to eight dollars an hour and his speech
improved immediately. He does the inventory and I let him do his
homework whenever we're not busy. He asked me for a smock the
other day, and I told him not to worry about it. I didn't mention I'd
set fire to them in a gasoline-soaked trash bucket. He needs to
shave now, and I ask him to do it before he comes to work. He usually does. If he needs a favor, he's always clean-shaven when he
asks for it. Sometimes, though, I see him looking at me, and I know
he knows something about the night I asked him to cover for me
until two in the morning. The kid isn't dumb.

Zorda comes by every now and then. He runs errands for Gardocki, and every time I see him, he is wearing a grin. He's got a
new leather jacket and he drives around all day in Gardocki's SUV.
The winter's over, and he usually has the CD player blaring and the
windows down when he comes in to ask for cigarettes. He's never
mentioned murdering anyone, but then, it's best not to. Even an
idiot like Jeff has figured that out. He mentions we should all go
to Tulley's when football season starts back up, and I think it
might actually happen. He wants to see the TV with the signal
which comes in ahead of the others. He still gets a kick out of that,
though we stay away from any mention of his uncontrollable sobbing and my pointing a pistol in his face.

Sheila's boyfriend is still alive, miraculously. If anyone deserved
a bullet it was that prick. I had to chase him away from my apartment with a shovel one afternoon after Sheila called me at the store.
She had just moved in with me, and she had come home from work
and found him waiting for her. He couldn't have cared less when
she first moved out, played it all cool, but after a few weeks he
started doing creepy shit, like slashing her tires. Tony Wolek told

me he finally took up with some nineteen-year-old girl and got her pregnant, so now he's got other things to think about. We haven't seen him in some time.

Speaking of pregnant, Sheila's doing well. We just found out last week. It might be time to get married soon, though it will have to be a Justice-of-the-Peace deal for now. There's no way I can take time off from the store for a honeymoon. Tommy would be working a hundred hours a week. Can't really afford a honeymoon right now, either. But being married would be nice. Every time I look at her, I think about how lucky I am.

It was my birthday last week, and I had to work the second shift, but Gardocki remembered it, of all people. He came into the store and gave me a handwritten gift certificate, instantly forgiving any losing bet up to and including one hundred dollars. What a sense of humor on that guy. Sheila doesn't want me gambling anymore, so that'll have to go in the trash. He also gave me a suitcase and told me to open it when I got home, not under the security camera. It was the sniper rifle from Miami, the one I never picked up. It's a beaut, all right. It comes apart into three pieces, and it has, get this . . . a silencer!